TIMBER!

TIMBER!

A Northwoods Story of Lumberjacks, Logging, and the Land

Susan Apps-Bodilly and Jerry Apps

Wisconsin Historical Society Press

Published by the **Wisconsin Historical Society Press**
Publishers since 1855

The Wisconsin Historical Society helps people connect to the past by collecting, preserving, and sharing stories. Founded in 1846, the Society is one of the nation's finest historical institutions.
Join the Wisconsin Historical Society: wisconsinhistory.org/membership

© 2024 by Susan R. Apps-Bodilly and Jerold W. Apps

Publication of this book was made possible in part from a grant from the Amy Louise Hunter fellowship fund.

For permission to reuse material from *Timber!* (ISBN 978-1-9766-0035-7; e-book ISBN 978-1-9766-0036-4), please access www.copyright.com or contact the Copyright Clearance Center, Inc. (CCC), 222 Rosewood Drive, Danvers, MA 01923, 978-750-8400. CCC is a not-for-profit organization that provides licenses and registration for a variety of users.

Photographs identified with WHI or WHS are from the Society's collections; address requests to reproduce these photos to the Visual Materials Archivist at the Wisconsin Historical Society, 816 State Street, Madison, WI 53706.

Front cover image, Jim Meyer; back cover images, WHI Image ID 78303 (top photo) and USDA Forest Service, Eastern Region (bottom photo).

This book is based in part on *When the White Pine Was King*, written by Jerry Apps and published by the Wisconsin Historical Society Press, 2020.

Printed in the United States of America
Initial design by Composure Graphics; additional design and layout by John Ferguson

28 27 26 25 24   1 2 3 4 5

Library of Congress Cataloging-in-Publication Data
Names: Apps-Bodilly, Susan, author. | Apps, Jerold W., 1934- author. | Apps, Jerold W., 1934– When the White pine was king. | Wisconsin Historical Society, publisher.
Title: Timber! : a Northwoods story of lumberjacks, logging, and the land / Susan Apps-Bodilly and Jerry Apps.
Description: [1st edition]. | Madison : Wisconsin Historical Society Press, 2024. | "This book is based in part on 'When the White Pine Was King', written by Jerry Apps and published by the Wisconsin Historical Society Press, 2020." | Includes bibliographical references and index. | Audience: Ages 10. | Audience: Grades 4–6.
Identifiers: LCCN 2024011389 (print) | LCCN 2024011390 (e-book) | ISBN 9781976600357 (paperback) | ISBN 9781976600364 (epub)
Subjects: LCSH: Logging—Wisconsin—History—Juvenile literature. | Loggers—Wisconsin—Juvenile literature. | Forests and forestry—Wisconsin—History—Juvenile literature. | Forest conservation—Wisconsin—Juvenile literature. | Wisconsin—History—Juvenile literature. | BISAC: JUVENILE NONFICTION / History / United States / State & Local | JUVENILE NONFICTION / Business & Economics
Classification: LCC HD9757.W5 A66 2024 (print) | LCC HD9757.W5 (e-book) | DDC 333.95/309755—dc23/eng/20240708
LC record available at https://lccn.loc.gov/2024011389
LC e-book record available at https://lccn.loc.gov/2024011390

∞ The paper used in this publication meets the minimum requirements of the American National Standard for Information Sciences—Permanence of Paper for Printed Library Materials, ANSI Z39.48-1992.

To the next generations of young people
responsible for caring for our forests.

Contents

Introduction... viii
1 Living with the Land.. 1
2 Early Settlers Choose Pine.. 8
3 Setting Up a Logging Camp... 13
4 Meet the Logging Crew.. 20
5 Feeding the Lumberjacks... 29
6 Work in the Woods... 37
7 When the Work Was Done... 46
8 The Log Drive.. 52
9 Challenge down the River... 61
10 From Logs to Lumber... 70
11 The Power of Steam... 80

12	The Dangers of Cutover Land	89
13	Restoring the Land	102
14	Forestry Today	116
15	The Future of the Forests	126
	Checklist	135
	Learn More	137
	Pronunciation Guide	142
	Glossary	144
	Acknowledgments	147
	Bibliography	148
	Illustration Credits	149
	Index	151

Introduction

The author as a child, sitting in a willow tree

When I was young, I climbed many trees. My family spent time at our tree farm. My favorite tree was a huge willow. This tree had been struck by lightning. One of its large branches bent down and touched the ground. It was the perfect sitting spot.

My dad tied a rope to a branch for us to swing from. We held the rope and jumped off, swinging and twirling around. One branch was injured, but the tree kept growing. It is still doing well today.

I also loved the white pines on the farm. Have you ever walked in a white pine forest? The branches whisper and rustle as the wind blows. A squirrel may scurry through. The birds sing. You can look up and see sunlight streaming through the branches.

Introduction ix

White pines were my favorite trees to climb. My brothers and I climbed up through the branches. We climbed until we were scared to go higher. We held onto the branches and looked around. My hands were covered in pine tree sap, and I usually scratched up my legs. But what a view!

White Pine Forests

This book tells the story of what happened in Wisconsin during the logging era. More than 200 years ago, this land was covered in trees. Forests of tall white pine covered the land.

The white pine forests of Wisconsin seemed to have an endless supply of trees. During the winters, lumberjacks lived and worked in the forest. They cut the giant pine trees into logs.

Logs were hauled away by oxen or horses and piled near the closest river. In the spring, the logs were floated down the river to the **sawmill**. At the sawmill, huge saws cut the logs into lumber. People near and far used that lumber to build houses and other buildings.

Logging continued until many forests were cut down. Decades of logging damaged the land. Many people wanted to protect the land and plant new trees. Many of them took action. Today, forests once again grow in Wisconsin and across the Upper Midwest.

> **Why did lumberjacks yell "Timber!" when cutting down trees?**
> Picture a man chopping down a tree. The tree begins to fall. The man yells "Timber!" to warn the other workers in the forest. This helped everyone stay safe when the tree came crashing down.

sawmill: a place where logs are sawed into boards and sold

Root for the Trees!

Do you have a favorite tree? It may be close to where you live. It may be on a school playground, in a park, or in a forest.

This book tells the story of how the great woods of Wisconsin provided for people in our past. Will you be someone who roots for trees in the future? Let's climb into the past and find out what happened. Then, go outside and find your favorite tree.

A trail winds through woods near Madison, Wisconsin.

Chapter 1

Living with the Land

Thousands of years ago, huge sheets of ice covered much of the land we now call Wisconsin. These sheets of ice were glaciers (**glay** shurz).

About 10,000 years ago, the weather began to change. The air got warmer. The glaciers began to melt and shrink. They left behind rich soil.

As the land warmed, trees began to grow. Some of the first trees to grow here were larch and spruce. These were followed by jack pine, red pine, and balsam fir.

About 8,000 years ago, white pine trees began to grow on this land. Over time, large forests covered the northern part of the entire Midwest.

Did you know?
As the glaciers melted, they formed the rivers, lakes, and bluffs that we see all over Wisconsin today!

Living with the Land

According to the origin stories of Native Nations, people have lived on this land since time began.

Early Native peoples lived along the edges of the receding glaciers. They moved as the seasons changed, following the animals. Over time, the **climate** (**clI** muht) got warmer. Some Native peoples began to stay in one place for longer periods of time.

Today, twelve Native Nations live in Wisconsin. They each have their own traditions and languages. One thing they all have in common is that their ancestors depended on the forests, lands, and waters to survive.

Native peoples hunted in the forests for deer, elk, and rabbits. They fished in the rivers and lakes. They **foraged** (**for** ijd) for plants, nuts, and wild berries. In the spring, they used sap from maple trees to make syrup.

Some Native groups, such as the Ojibwe (oh **jib** way) and Menominee (muh **nah** muh nee), harvested wild rice in northern Wisconsin waters. Some groups, such as the Ho-Chunk (**hoh** chuhnk), also grew corn, beans, squash, and other crops.

Native peoples did not think of the land as something that belonged to only one person. They shared what they gathered, fished, and hunted with other members of their Nation.

Native peoples used trees from the forest to build canoes. Some built dugout canoes out of huge tree trunks. Others built lighter canoes from the bark of birch trees. They used the canoes for fishing and travel. The oldest canoe ever found in the Great Lakes region is 4,500 years old!

They also used trees to build their homes. For example, the Woodland people lived more than 2,000 years ago. They used

---

climate: the average condition of the weather over time

foraged: searched for food

young trees called saplings to build shelters. The sapling poles were lashed together and covered with woven mats or bark.

Native Nations lived on the land we now call Wisconsin long before Europeans arrived. They **adapted** (uh **dap** tid) their way of life to the environment, for thousands of years. They took care of the forests, lands, and waterways for future generations. They believed the land should be treated with respect. This is a belief that Native peoples still have today.

adapted: changed or adjusted to fit different conditions

An Ojibwe woman and man work together to build a canoe out of wood and bark. This painting was made by Bad River Ojibwe artist Peter Whitebird.

Europeans Arrive

French explorers were the first Europeans to travel to the Midwest. They came during the late 1600s.

The French were looking for river routes to the west and south. They also were looking for land, animal pelts, and people to trade with.

The Midwest had many lakes and rivers. The forests and waterways were full of animals, especially beavers. Beaver pelts were soft, warm, and waterproof. People in Europe loved hats and coats made from beaver pelts.

Native peoples knew how to trap the beavers. The French traded **goods** like knives, kettles, and wool blankets in exchange for beaver pelts. They sent the pelts back to France.

People from Great Britain came to the region starting in the 1750s. They also wanted beaver pelts. They traded with Native peoples, too. The French and British wanted so many pelts that almost all the beavers were killed.

More Settlers Arrive

By the 1830s, thousands of white settlers began to arrive in the southwestern part of what we now call Wisconsin.

Some settlers came from eastern US states. Others came from Germany, Norway, and other European countries.

Many settlers were farmers. They knew about Wisconsin's good climate and rich soil. They wanted to use the land to farm.

But there was a problem. When the settlers arrived, the land was covered in forests of giant trees. Some trees were 300 years old! The settlers wanted to farm, but the forests were in the way.

> **goods**: things that are made to be sold or traded

Living with the Land   5

This painting by Lavern Kammerude shows how neighbors worked together to saw wood.

Settlers cleared the land by cutting the giant trees. They used some of the wood to build log cabins and barns. They used wood fires for cooking. They also used fires to stay warm during the long, cold winters.

Settlers cut down more trees than they needed. They often burned the extra wood. Smoke filled the air for miles as trees were cut and burned. Settlers in southern Wisconsin worked hard to rid the land of trees.

Changes to the Land

In the early 1800s, thousands of Native people lived on the land that would become Wisconsin. The US government wanted Native Nations to give up their lands. The government wanted to take Native land and turn it into territories and states. The US government used treaties (**tree** teez) to force Native people to move. A treaty is an agreement between nations. Treaties describe certain rights and rules.

These treaties were unfair to Native Nations. The US government did not always explain to Native people what the treaties meant. Native people often didn't realize the federal government would own the land. They did not know the government would sell the land to settlers.

The United States did not live up to the promises it made in its treaties. The government used treaties to force many Native Nations to move to unfamiliar places far from their homes. Often, Native people no longer had access to the waterways and forests they needed for survival.

Wisconsin became a **territory** in 1836. At that time, the Menominee people lived in the eastern and central parts of the territory. In 1836, the US government signed a treaty with the Menominee Nation. The treaty forced the Menominee people to cede (**seed**), or give up, half of their land and waters.

territory: a piece of land that belongs to the US but is not a state

In 1837, the US government forced the Ho-Chunk, Ojibwe, and Dakota Nations to sign treaties. These treaties allowed the US government to take more Native lands.

Wisconsin became a state in 1848. That same year, the government pressured the Menominee to give up even more of their land. The US government now owned most of the northern forests of Wisconsin.

The government **surveyed** (**sur** vayd) and mapped the land in northern Wisconsin. Over time, the government divided the land and sold it to non-Native people.

Northern Wisconsin was known for its forests and rivers. Soon logging companies looked to these forests to cut trees and sell timber. The pine forests would provide the wood that new settlers wanted.

surveyed: examined the condition or value

Chapter 2

Early Settlers Choose Pine

Thousands of settlers came to Wisconsin in the 1800s. Towns began to form. Residents needed to build homes, barns, schools, and stores. They needed lumber.

Lumber is made when timber is sawed into boards. Settlers needed lumber for all sorts of things. They used lumber for every part of buildings: the frame, floors, siding, window frames, doors, and roof shingles. They used lumber to make tables, chairs, desks, beds, baby cradles, and other furniture. They used lumber for barns and sheds. They used lumber to build sidewalks, bridges, and fences.

Many kinds of trees can be made into lumber. Settlers liked white pine lumber the best. White pines were easy to cut with hand tools. White pines were tall and straight. White pine lumber was soft but tough. It was perfect for building houses. It made sturdy walls and floors. It made strong roof shingles. White pine was the tree of choice.

Timber vs. Lumber
Timber is raw wood that hasn't been processed (**prah** sest)—like a tree right after it's cut down. *Lumber* is wood that has been cut into boards or pieces—like the pieces of wood used to build a house.

Early Settlers Choose Pine   9

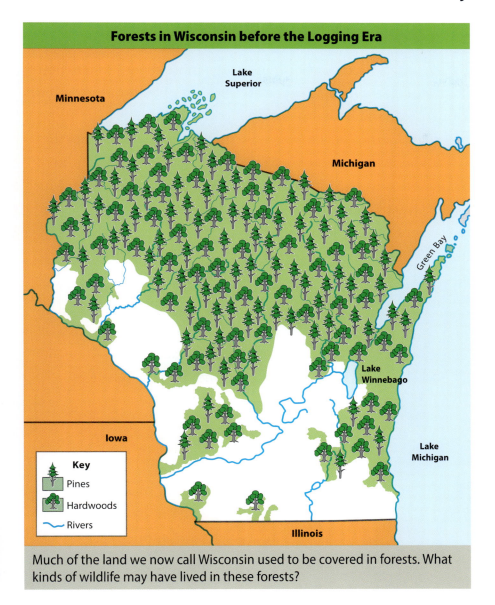

Much of the land we now call Wisconsin used to be covered in forests. What kinds of wildlife may have lived in these forests?

Settlers loved white pine for another reason. White pine logs float in water! This is how logging companies moved the heavy logs to the sawmills.

The Demand for White Pine Grows

By the time Wisconsin became a state, more than 300,000 non-Native people lived in Wisconsin. More people from the eastern United States and Europe moved to Wisconsin.

Thousands of people were also moving farther west, into the Great Plains. The Great Plains is a huge area. It stretches from Minnesota west to Montana, and all the way south to Texas. Much of the Great Plains is flatland. Fewer trees grew there. Settlers in the Great Plains needed lumber from Midwestern forests.

Two men saw a tree in the winter of 1890.

Cities needed lumber, too. Cities like Chicago and St. Louis were growing quickly. People needed lumber to build more houses and buildings. People in many parts of the country purchased their wood from Wisconsin.

Logging Begins

People who owned logging companies saw a way to make a lot of money. They would cut trees in the vast forests that grew across northern Minnesota, Wisconsin, and Michigan.

White pines grew well in Wisconsin's climate and soil. Wisconsin's white pines were huge! They grew to be more than 75 feet tall. Some grew to be 120 feet tall! They were almost three feet wide or more. Some white pine trees were 200 years old. Sixteen to 20 huge pine trees could grow in one acre (**ay** kur) of forest.

Logging company owners knew settlers needed and wanted pine lumber. They knew millions of white pines grew in northern Wisconsin. And they knew they could use Wisconsin's many rivers to move the logs to the sawmills.

In the 1840s, logging companies began setting up logging camps and sawmills. Soon, the sound of axes filled the Northwoods. Workers were cutting trees and making lumber. For many years, logging stayed mostly the same.

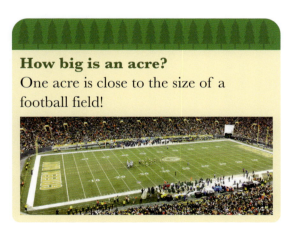

How big is an acre?
One acre is close to the size of a football field!

Timber!

Deciduous and Coniferous Trees

Do you know the difference between a deciduous (di **si** juh wuhs) tree and a coniferous (koh **ni** fur es) tree?

Deciduous trees have leaves that fall off in autumn. Deciduous trees grow slowly. Their wood is dense and strong. Examples of deciduous trees are maple, oak, and birch.

Coniferous trees have needles and cones. The needles stay green all winter. These trees are called evergreens.

Coniferous trees grow quickly. Their wood is lighter and less dense. They are easier to cut. Examples of coniferous trees are pine, spruce, and fir.

Deciduous trees in autumn

Coniferous trees in winter

Chapter 3

Setting Up a Logging Camp

Logging companies had to buy land before they could set up logging camps.

By the mid-1800s, the US government had signed many treaties with Native Nations in the Great Lakes region. Over time, these treaties allowed the government to take millions of acres of Native land and sell it to non-Native people.

Much of this land was purchased by logging companies. A single logging company could buy thousands of acres of forest land.

The Timber Cruiser

Logging companies sent workers into the Northwoods to decide if a piece of land was worth buying. These workers were called "timber cruisers" (**kroo** zurz).

The timber cruisers looked at the land. They made sure it would be good for logging. Timber cruisers worked alone or in

Timber!

Timber Cruiser Math

Logging was a business. The owners wanted to make a profit (**prah** fit). Timber cruisers needed to estimate how much lumber the company could get from the land. To do this, they needed math.

Here is how a timber cruiser estimated how much lumber an area of forest could produce:

A white pine forest

1. He measured an area that was 200 feet by 200 feet. That was 40,000 square feet, or almost an acre.
2. He counted or estimated how many trees were in the marked off area.
3. He estimated how many board feet could be cut from one tree. A board foot is a piece of lumber that is one foot wide, one foot long, and one inch thick.
4. He multiplied the number of trees in the marked off area by the number of board feet per tree. This gave him the total feet of lumber that one acre of trees could produce. This is the equation he used:

Number of trees × board feet per tree = Total feet of lumber

The answer helped the logging company decide whether it wanted to buy the land.

The best timber cruisers did not need to use math to estimate timber. They simply climbed up a tree and looked out at part of the forest. By looking at the trees, they determined how many board feet an area would produce.

Here is a math problem for you:

The timber cruiser counts 200 trees. An average tree contains 50 board feet. How many board feet could be harvested from the trees he counted?

Check your answer at the end of this chapter.

Setting Up a Logging Camp 15

small groups. They traveled by river to get to the forest. They slept in tents and did their own cooking. Timber cruisers earned up to $3.50 a day. This was a good wage in the late 1800s.

Building the Logging Camp

After the lumber company purchased the land, it was time to build the logging camp.

First, a small crew chose the best place to set up the camp. The camp needed to be close to the trees they wanted to cut. It needed to be near a river so the crew could float logs to the

Men, women, and children pose in the snow outside of a logging camp near Black River Falls, Wisconsin.

sawmill. The river also gave them fresh water for cooking and drinking.

The crew cut, or felled (**feld**), trees to make room for a main road. This road went from the camp to the river. They cut other roads to the cutting sites.

Workers felled more trees to make room for the camp buildings. The buildings were made of big logs. They had waterproof roofs made of tarpaper.

The buildings were not meant to last a long time. When the logging crew finished cutting trees in one area, they moved on to the next part of the forest.

Early logging camps needed only a few buildings. They had one building for workers and one building for oxen. Over time, camps got bigger. Larger camps had many buildings.

What do you think it was like to share a bunkhouse with so many people?

Bunkhouse

The crew slept in the bunkhouse. This was a building with one large room. Bunk beds lined the walls. The crew slept on prickly mattresses filled with hay. Sometimes 30 or more men slept in one room.

A woodstove in the center kept the room warm.

The buildings in a logging camp

Lanterns provided light. There was a small table where the crew could play cards or write letters. They used a water barrel and metal pans or bowls to wash their hands and faces.

Outhouse

An outhouse is a small structure used for going to the bathroom. Inside was a wooden bench with one or two holes. The bench was built over a hole in the ground. An outhouse did not have running water.

Barn

The oxen or horses slept and ate in the barn. Sometimes the crew also built a shed to store hay for the animals.

Timber!

Lumberjacks eat a big meal inside the cookhouse.

Cookhouse

The cook made all the meals in the cookhouse. This is also where the crew ate. They sat at long tables with benches on either side. The cook's sleeping room was in this building.

Blacksmith Shop

The blacksmith shop is where the blacksmith worked. The blacksmith made and repaired the logging tools. The blacksmith shop had a special kind of fireplace called a forge (**forj**). The forge was used to heat metal. The blacksmith put the red-hot metal on an **anvil**. Then the blacksmith used a hammer to shape the metal into a tool. A water barrel cooled the metal after it was shaped. A bin held extra **coal** (**kohl**) to keep the fire burning.

Store

The camp store was small and simple. The crew could buy clothes, boots, and mittens. They could buy needles and thread to mend holes in their socks and clothes.

anvil: a heavy block made of iron

coal: a solid black mineral that is mined and used for fuel

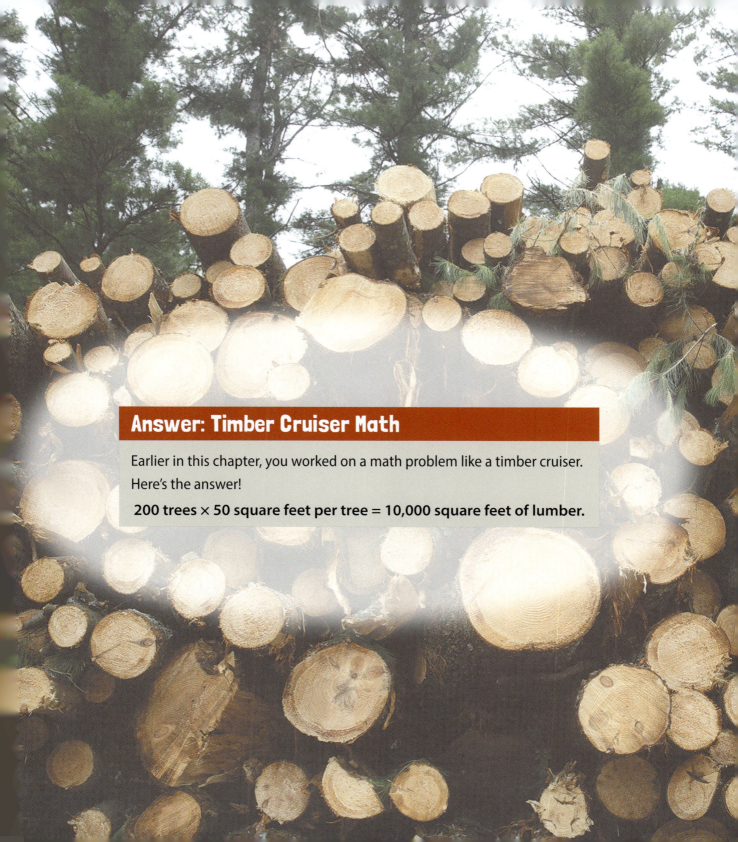

Answer: Timber Cruiser Math

Earlier in this chapter, you worked on a math problem like a timber cruiser. Here's the answer!

200 trees × 50 square feet per tree = 10,000 square feet of lumber.

Chapter 4

Meet the Logging Crew

Logging was a team effort. The crew and the animals worked together. Workers left their families at home for the winter. They lived and worked in the woods.

A logging camp was a busy place. When logging started in the 1840s, about 25 people lived and worked in a single camp. By the late 1800s, some logging camps had 100 workers or more.

Who Worked in a Logging Camp?

Most logging camp workers were men. They came from many places. Many workers were **immigrants** from Europe. They brought logging skills they learned in their homelands.

Some workers came to the Midwest from logging camps in Canada, Maine, and northern New York. These men were experienced loggers. Now they could use their skills in the Midwest.

immigrants: people from one country who move to live in another

Meet the Logging Crew

Winter in the Forest

Why did lumberjacks work in the winter? Cold winter months were ideal for cutting logs.

- The snow and frozen ground made it easier to move the logs. Oxen or horses pulled a sled full of logs over the snow. In the summer, muddy swamps and other wet areas could trap workers and animals. In the winter, they traveled more easily.
- Farmers were available to work during the winter season.
- There were no insects, such as mosquitoes, in the woods during the winter.
- Snow melts in the spring and flows into rivers. When a river is full, the water can move quickly. This made it easier to float the logs down the river to the sawmill.

Other workers were new to logging. They had to be strong and willing to learn. For some workers, the job gave them a sense of adventure. For others, it was a good way to earn money for their families.

Some logging camps had pets. Can you spot the lumberjack holding a cat in this picture?

People of many ages worked on logging crews. Some workers were as young as 16 years old. The more experienced workers taught the younger workers. Everyone worked together to make things run smoothly.

Jobs in a Logging Crew

In early logging camps, most lumberjacks did a variety of jobs. As camps got bigger, each person was assigned to one job. That kept the camp running smoothly.

Barn Boss

The barn boss made sure the barn was clean. The barn boss also took care of all the animals. Camps had oxen or horses. Some camps also had a cow that provided milk for cooking.

Blacksmith

The blacksmith made the saws, hammers, and other logging tools. When a tool broke, the blacksmith could fix it. The blacksmith also made horseshoes for the horses. All of these things were made out of metal, such as iron or steel. The blacksmith used a process called forging. Forging involves heating metal and then bending the metal into different shapes. The metal got very hot. Sparks often flew! The blacksmith wore a leather apron to keep from getting burned.

A blacksmith removes a shoe from a horse at a logging camp in Forest County, Wisconsin.

Bookkeeper or Clerk

Bookkeepers and clerks kept track of how many hours the crew worked. They figured out how much the crew should get paid. They also ran the camp store. When workers purchased something from the store, the cost was taken out of their pay. Logging crew workers received their pay at the end of the logging season in the spring.

Cook

The cook made the meals for the crew. The cook's job was very important. Lumberjacks might leave and find work in a different camp if the food wasn't good enough. Some workers returned each winter to the camp where a favorite cook worked.

Cookee

The cookee was the person who helped the cook. The cookee set the tables, served the food, and washed the dishes. Cookees hauled water, carried firewood, and cleaned the cookhouse.

Foreman

The foreman was the boss of the entire camp. Sometimes the foreman was married and had children. The family lived together in a separate building. Usually the foreman had worked as a lumberjack when he was younger.

The foreman hired all the camp's workers. He supervised the crew each day.

The foreman kept order in the camp. He handled conflicts and made sure people followed the rules. In some camps, pay could be taken away if a worker broke a rule.

Lumberjack

Lumberjacks cut the trees. There were many kinds of lumberjacks:

- The **fitter** decided which way a tree should fall. The fitter used an axe to chop a V-shaped notch into the tree. The notch showed which direction the tree was going to fall.
- The **choppers** felled the trees. They used huge saws. The saws were so big that one person had to hold each end.
- After the tree was felled, a **sawyer** used an axe or saw to cut off the limbs and branches.
- Finally, the **bucker** used a saw to cut the logs into the right lengths for the sawmill.

Two lumberjacks fell a giant tree.

Marker

The marker stamped a mark into each log. The mark was a small symbol. Each company had its own mark.

Saw Filer

The saw filer took care of the saws, axes, and other tools that had blades. The saw filer sharpened the blades so lumberjacks could do their best work.

Scaler

The scaler counted and measured each log. The scaler checked the logs for rotten spots. This made sure only good quality logs were sent to the sawmill.

Skidder

The skidder moved logs to the river after they were cut. The skidder used horses, tools, and sleds to move the logs.

Swamper

The swamper made and repaired the paths that cut through the woods. Workers used these paths to drive sleds full of heavy logs to an area near the frozen river. The swamper cut away brush in the woods to keep the paths clear.

Teamster

The teamster drove the team of animals that pulled the sleds. In the early logging years, oxen pulled the sleds. Oxen were powerful and strong, but they were slow-moving.

By the 1850s, loggers used draft horses instead of oxen. Draft horses were large and strong. They were faster and easier to care for than oxen.

Some crews used oxen *and* horses. This crew worked near Big Falls, Wisconsin, in about 1900.

How Much Did They Get Paid?

In the late 1800s, most lumberjacks earned 26 to 30 dollars a month. This was a good wage at the time.

The highest paid worker in a logging camp was the foreman. He earned up to 100 dollars a month. Cooks earned 40 to 45 dollars a month. Cookees earned 18 to 22 dollars a month. A teamster in charge of a two-horse team was paid 24 to 28 dollars a month. A teamster in charge of a four-horse team earned 32 to 35 dollars a month.

Each job included three meals a day and a place to sleep.

Primary Source

What Is a Primary Source?

Historians use primary sources to study the past. A primary source is something that was written or made during the time that is being studied. It can be a letter, a photograph, a map, a newspaper article, a written or recorded memory, or another kind of **artifact** (**ar** ti fakt).

Primary sources show us how people lived, acted, and felt. They help us explore the ways our lives are different from or similar to the way people lived in the past. When examining a primary source, think about where it came from, who made it, and why it was made.

artifact: an object from a particular time period

Meet the Logging Crew 27

Primary Source

Letter from a Lumberjack

John Ziebarth became a lumberjack when he was 16 years old. He was from Green Bay, Wisconsin. He worked in logging camps in Michigan and Wisconsin. In 1899, John wrote this letter to his family:

Mich. [Michigan] 1899, December 17th

Dear Father and Mother,
I got your kind and welcome letter the 1 [first] of Dec. I think you are all expecting a letter. I am getting along alright, and I hope you were the same. We had a big snowstorm Monday and it lasted all day. I have 34 working days in. I don't think of coming down [for] Christmas. . . . They are going to start hauling after new years.

   The fellow that used to sleep near me jumped [quit work] Monday and helped himself to my drawers [underwear] and a pair of mitts [mittens]. You need not trouble your self by sending anything down. I will see that I dress with that I got [what I have]. It aint very cold in the daytime but heavy frost at night. They are going to have two seigen [skidding] teams at work all winter. I have had no kick [complaint] yet. I like the board [living conditions and food] and it aint so very hard work. I don't think you will know me in spring for I am gaining [growing] very fast. I expect to stay hear [here] till in spring. I think I will close my letter now for I have not much to say. But all I said is to let you know that I am well and I hope you were that same. When writing me a letter send me the news and tell me if all the rest of the boys is to home. I bid farewell with all my best regards to you all Father and Mother. So goodbye to you all. You need not expect me Christmas for I am going to stay here.

After reading:

What does the letter tell you about John?

What was John's purpose for writing the letter?

What does John's letter tell you about working in a logging camp? Do you think he was being truthful? Why or why not?

If you could talk to John, what questions would you ask him?

Lumberjacks pose with their logs at a camp near Antigo, Wisconsin. Do you notice that they're wearing dress clothes? Why do you think that is?

Chapter 5
Feeding the Lumberjacks

It was January 1875 at a logging camp deep in the Northwoods. Winter mornings were dark and cold. The cook and cookee woke up at 3:00 a.m. They started making a huge breakfast on the wood-burning stove in the cookhouse.

At 4:00 a.m., the cookee woke up the teamsters. The teamsters fed, brushed, and harnessed the horses.

Then, at 4:30 a.m., it was time to wake the lumberjacks.

The cookee opened the door to the bunkhouse. The temperature outside was 20 degrees below zero. Frost covered the inside of the bunkhouse's log walls.

"Breakfast on the table!" the cookee yelled.

Slowly, 35 lumberjacks crawled out of their bunks to face another day in the woods.

The lumberjacks pulled on warm clothing. First they put on long underwear. Then they put on wool shirts and pants. They held up their pants with suspenders. They wore red socks pulled

A logging crew in Sawyer County, Wisconsin, in about 1911.

up to their knees. Sometimes they needed more than one pair of socks to keep their feet warm. They wore boots, hats, and heavy wool coats called Mackinaws (**mah** ki nawz).

While the lumberjacks got dressed, the cook and cookee made sure the food was ready. The lumberjacks needed a healthy meal before working in the woods. The work day could last for 12 hours. They worked in freezing, wet weather. A big breakfast was an important part of their day.

The Camp Cook and Cookee

For most lumberjacks, getting three big meals each day was the best part of the job. A good camp cook made a happy logging crew. A bad cook created a grumpy crew that constantly complained.

People still wear Mackinaws. This kind of coat is made of thick and heavy wool material. It usually has a black and red checkered pattern.

A cook and cookee prepare a meal in the cookhouse. They worked at a logging camp near Hayward, Wisconsin.

Cooks worked long hours every day. They made all the food on a wood-burning stove or an open fire outside. The cook and cookee used heavy cooking pots made of cast iron. They cooked all the food from scratch.

People in Wisconsin did not have electricity until the 1880s. Without electricity, there were no refrigerators. Logging camps used snow and ice to keep things cold.

Vegetables were kept in a root cellar or in a building called a root house. The root house was built partly underground. It was covered in soil to keep out frost. This protected the vegetables from freezing during the winter. The air inside the root house was cool so the vegetables wouldn't rot.

Getting Food into the Woods

Logging camps were often deep in the woods. This made it challenging to provide enough food for the workers and animals.

Each fall, tote wagons were loaded with food and supplies in the nearest town. Horses pulled the wagons all the way to the logging camps.

Some parts of the Northwoods had many camps. As many as 50 tote wagons might travel along the same road delivering supplies!

Primary Source

Memories of the Tote Wagon

A lumberjack named William Alft worked at a logging camp on the Wolf River in 1896. This is a memory he shared several years later:

> With many camps scattered along the river . . . there was need for an unusual supply of food and clothing for men; hay and oats for the horses. Each camp had at least one tote team traveling from Shawano to the camps. In the fall, forty to fifty four-horse teams hauled supplies on this busy road. Sometimes . . . a wagon broke down or a horse was injured on the road, and a load of supplies was several days late. When this happened, the camp ran out of supplies, and I can remember when all we had to eat was boiled potatoes, syrup, and pancakes. We used to go out of camp in the evening and listen for the tote wagon to come in, and what a welcome sound it was to hear the rattle of the wagon.

After reading:

What do William's memories tell you about working in a logging camp?

What do you think made events like this memorable?

When wagons couldn't bring supplies on time, how might that have affected the logging crew? How might it affect the logging business?

Feeding the Lumberjacks

What Was on the Menu?

Logging crews ate three big meals every day: breakfast in the morning, dinner at noon, and supper at night. A typical day's menu might look like this:

Breakfast

Pancakes
Oatmeal mush
Rye bread, cornbread and syrup, donuts
Cornmeal cookies with apple butter
Creamed potatoes
Codfish cakes
Coffee

Dinner

Rice and tomato soup
Roast beef and gravy
Mashed potatoes
Bread and butter
Boiled onions with corn
Apricot rolls with blackberry jam

Supper

Potato salad
Baked beans
Corn with gravy
Nut bread and butter
Stewed prunes and molasses cookies

Lumberjacks used simple metal dishes. They were lightweight and strong. If you have ever gone camping, you may have used plates or cups that looked like these!

Dinner at a logging camp, in about 1885

Women in the Logging Camp

In the late 1800s, few women worked in logging camps. Some people believed that living and working in the woods was too hard for women.

However, historic photographs show us that women did live and work in logging camps. By the late 1890s, women worked in logging camps as cooks and cookees. In some camps, children also helped with the cooking and cleaning.

A woman named Iva Trotier was a logging camp cook. Iva worked at a camp with her sister-in-law Mary. Iva's husband worked on the logging crew. Iva had a young baby. Iva, Mary, and the baby moved to the logging camp in the winter of 1910. Iva and Mary worked at the camp until late spring.

Two women and their children at a Wisconsin logging camp

Feeding the Lumberjacks

Primary Source

Iva Trotier's Own Words

Iva Trotier wrote about her job as a camp cook. Her article appeared in the *Rhinelander Daily News*:

> It was October 1910, and my husband hired out for the winter . . . for a logging job. At the time he said they needed a cook and a helper. We applied for the job . . . After seeming to be a long drive, lo and behold, we came out into a clearing on top of a little knoll [a small hill], and below us on a level spot was our home to be for the winter. I will never forget it. There below us was a long log building under one roof, a cook shanty, office and men's shanty. There was also a horse barn, a root cellar and meat house, tool shed and two little outhouses. . . . Running so peacefully nearby was a big creek and a lovely spring for drinking water. We unloaded and had four days to get organized before the crew came in. . . . There were tables and benches. Many of the provisions were packed in old-fashioned orange crates with the dividers in, so they were nailed to the log walls and served as cabinets. Mary slept on a folding cot, which when not in use was shoved under our bed. Our bedroom had two log walls, the end and one side. . . . The door was curtained with two gunny sacks [sacks made from rough fabric] sewed together. There was just enough room for our bunk, the baby's crib, a small chest, and two orange crates nailed to the wall. The first night we worked late filling shelves and finding where things were. We found the office also

was the storage building. In it were sacks of sugar, flour, beans, peas, rice, macaroni, coffee, raisins, dried apples, apricots and the like. There were also tobacco, cigarettes, matches, wool socks, and mitts for the men to buy when they ran short. Also in the cook shanty was a barrel of sauerkraut and half a barrel of dill pickles, a large assortment of unhemmed dishtowels made of flour sacks and plenty of dishrags. We made out our menus for a week and set to work. The dishes were all [made] of tin . . . so there was no dish breakage. As soon as the dishes were washed after a meal, the table was set, ready for the next meal. . . . We baked ten loaves of bread every other day, besides making light cake, dark cake, raised doughnuts, fried cakes, cookies, bread pudding and pies. Thank heaven my little son was a good baby. We made a makeshift playpen out of a large box, put a blanket in the bottom, and put in his toys, and there he played unless he was hungry or needed other attention. He spent his first birthday in camp.

After reading:

What does this article tell you about Iva? What worries did she express? How might you have felt in her shoes?

Do you think Iva's article changed some people's minds about women working in logging camps? Why or why not?

What do you think it was like for a one-year-old to live in a logging camp?

Chapter 6

Work in the Woods

Lumberjacks worked from sunrise until sunset. After breakfast, the teamsters and animals set off for the woods. The lumberjacks soon followed. Sometimes they walked a mile or more in near darkness. They arrived at the cutting site just before sunrise.

Felling the Trees

The lumberjack's main job was felling, or cutting down, trees. Felling trees was a dangerous and difficult job.

In the early days of logging, lumberjacks felled trees with axes. After the 1870s, they also used a special kind of saw called a crosscut saw. Lumberjacks used crosscut saws that were even longer than the tree was wide.

The first step in felling a tree was to decide which

Axes

Lumberjacks used different axes for different purposes. A single-bitted axe has one cutting edge. A double-bitted axe has two cutting edges, one on each side. These axes were used to fell trees and remove limbs. Other kinds of axes were used to break up big rocks or cut the edges of logs.

> **Crosscut saw**
>
> The crosscut saw was used to fell trees and cut them into logs. Two people were needed to use a crosscut saw. One person stood on each end.

way it should fall. Lumberjacks figured out how a tree should fall so it wouldn't hit the crew, horses, or other trees. This was called "reading a tree." In a forest full of tall pine trees, knowing how to read a tree was a very important skill.

Next, the fitter used an axe to cut a big V-shaped notch into the trunk of the tree. The notch marked the direction the lumberjack wanted the tree to fall.

After the tree was notched, two lumberjacks held each end of a crosscut saw. They sawed on the side of the tree opposite the notch. They sawed for several minutes before the tree started to fall. When the saw reached the notch, the tree leaned toward the notch. As the huge trunk began to break, a loud crack echoed across the pineland.

When the tree started falling, the lumberjacks quickly stepped back and yelled "Timber!" Everyone in the woods ran out of the way when they heard this warning. The big pine tree landed with a tremendous crash!

With the tree safely on the ground, sawyers used axes or saws to remove the limbs from the trunk.

Next, lumberjacks used a crosscut saw to cut the tree trunk into logs. Sawing a felled tree into logs was called "bucking." The logs were cut to different lengths: 12, 14, or 16 feet long. Sawmills needed different lengths for different purposes. Many logs were cut from one giant tree trunk.

Lumberjacks usually didn't use the very top part of the tree. The top of the tree often had too many branches to remove. Lumber from the top of the tree had too many knots. Knots are where branches connect to the tree trunk. Many times, the top of the tree was left in the woods.

Two lumberjacks are about to use a crosscut saw to fell a tall tree.

How tall were the trees?
White pines could grow 150 feet tall. How tall is that? A stop sign is 10 feet tall. Imagine 15 stop signs stacked end to end. That is the height of a 150-foot-tall tree.

Skidding the Trees

To skid logs means to drag them from the cutting site to the river. The person who did this was the skidder.

The skidder used skidding tongs to move the logs. One end of the tongs hooked around the log. The other end of the tongs

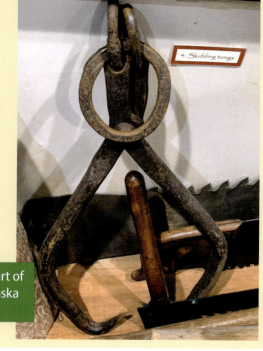

Skidding tongs

Skidding tongs were big metal hooks that could open and close. They could open up to 32 inches wide. They were used to grab and hold logs. They looked like giant ice tongs!

These skidding tongs were part of a logging display at the Onalaska Area Historical Museum.

had a chain. The chain was connected to a horse's harness. The horse pulled the log out of the woods.

Some logs were too big for the tongs. The crew used a go-devil sled to skid these logs out of the woods.

The crew put one end of the log onto the go-devil sled. An ox or a horse pulled the go-devil sled through the woods. As the sled was pulled, the back half of the log skidded along the ground.

The crew needed a wide trail to skid the huge logs. The swampers kept the trails clear of brush and rocks. The trails cut through the woods and led to a logging road.

Go-devil

A go-devil was a small sled with two wooden runners. It was used to haul big logs to the logging road.

Work in the Woods   41

Loading the Bobsled

Workers skidded one log at a time, from the cutting site to the logging road. Then they loaded the logs onto bobsleds.

The crew leaned two logs against one side of the sled to make a ramp. A team of horses stood on the opposite side of the sled.

The crew piled logs on the ground at the bottom of the ramp. They tied one end of a rope to the logs on the ground.

This painting by Carl Arneson shows a logging scene from the 1890s. A team of oxen skids a log. In the background, two sawyers use a crosscut saw to cut a massive tree. Another lumberjack stands on a tree stump. He will use his axe to trim the branches once the tree falls.

A crew loads logs onto a horse-drawn sled. This picture was taken near Rib Lake, Wisconsin, in 1911.

Bobsled

A bobsled helped the crew get the logs to the river. Bobsleds were much bigger than go-devils. A bobsled held a large pile of logs. Two teams of horses pulled the bobsled from the woods to the riverbank.

Cant hook

A cant hook is five feet long. It is a wooden pole with a movable metal hook at the end. It was used for lifting, turning, and moving logs.

They tied the other end of rope to the team of horses. The horses moved forward and slowly pulled the log up the ramp. The crew used metal poles called cant hooks to guide the log onto the sled.

The first log was placed in the center of the bobsled. Workers chained the next logs into position on either side of the first log. As they added more logs, the load grew higher.

A man stood on the top to help guide each log into place. Sometimes, this person was called the skybird because he worked so far above the ground. This job required skill and balance.

Once the sled was loaded, chains held the logs in place. Oxen or horses pulled the bobsled down the road to the river.

Work in the Woods 43

The Logging Road

Ice often covered the logging roads in the winter. Hauling logs on an icy road was dangerous.

The crew built logging roads as level as possible. Sometimes they couldn't avoid building a road on a hill. It was challenging for teamsters to control the horses on hilly roads covered in ice. If a sled moved too fast, it tipped over. The logs fell off the sled. A sled could run off the road and get stuck in the snow!

Some logging crews hired a worker called a hay-man-on-the-hill. This person used hay or sand to cover the steep, hilly roads. This helped the sleds slow down.

The hay man did his work before the rest of the crew arrived for the day. He worked in the dark and used a lantern. He made sure the logging road was safe for the men and animals.

Piling the Logs at the River

Finally, the sleds arrived at the frozen river.

To "deck up" means to pile logs along a riverbank. This was perhaps the most dangerous job on a logging crew.

The crew used ropes, chains, and a **pulley** system to lift the logs off the bobsled. A worker called a top decker carefully steered each log into place on the big pile. If a log swung too far or too fast, it could hit the top decker and injure him.

The logs would stay in the pile until the river melted in the spring.

pulley: a tool used to lift or lower heavy objects

Measuring the Logs

A log scaler worked at the decking site on the riverbank. He estimated how many board feet could be cut from each log at the mill.

The scaler counted, measured, and examined every log. He took notes about the quality of the logs. He reported the results to the logging company owner. The owner used this information to estimate the value of the logs.

Marking the Logs

Early in the logging season, the blacksmith made a cast iron stamp of the company's log mark.

Each logging company had its own mark. Some marks were the owner's initials. Other marks were simple shapes or pictures.

The logs were marked once they reached the river. The person who did this was the marker. He put the mark on the end or side of the logs with a stamping hammer.

Each log was marked several times. Logs owned by many companies floated on the same rivers. The marks helped workers know which logs belonged to which company.

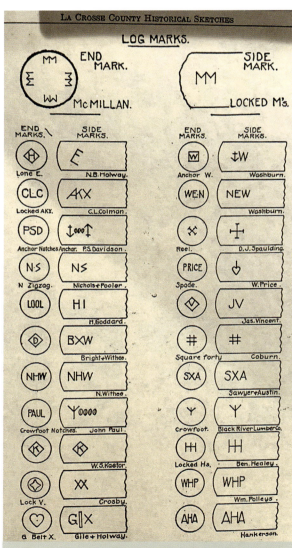

These were some of the logging marks used by logging companies on the Black River. Logs were marked on the ends and sides.

Work in the Woods   45

These logs were marked with "OJCH." These may have been the initials of the logging company owner.

Sunup to Sundown

Logging crews worked long days. Some days they worked close to camp. They could go back to the cookhouse for lunch.

On other days, they worked too far away to eat lunch at camp. The cook used sleds to carry hot food deep into the forest. The cook started a fire to warm up the crew's tea or coffee. Lumberjacks ate their lunch in the woods and then kept working.

They worked until it was too dark to cut trees. The crew returned to the logging camp. They went to the bunkhouse and removed their boots. They hung their wet clothes near the stove to dry. They washed up in pans of water. Supper would be ready soon.

Meanwhile, piles of logs waited for the spring thaw at the river's edge.

Chapter 7

When the Work Was Done

A lumberjack relaxes by reading a book. This picture was taken at a logging camp in Minnesota in 1914.

Lumberjacks spent long days working in the woods. They worked six days a week. They did not work on Sundays. What did they do when they were not working?

In the evening, the lumberjacks went back to the bunkhouse. They sewed patches over rips in their pants. They darned (**dahrnd**) their socks. They read books by the light of an oil lantern. Some played card games. Some rested on their bunks. The smell of wet wool clothes drying by the stove filled the room.

 What does it mean to darn a sock? To darn fabric means to mend a hole with a needle and thread. Lumberjacks would darn their socks instead of throwing them away.

46

Playing Music

In the evening, the tired lumberjacks entertained themselves with music. Lumberjacks enjoyed singing as a group. They sang lumberjack songs about impressive logging work or about family back home. They often made up their own songs!

Some men brought a fiddle, guitar, or harmonica to camp. However, most of the time, they sang without instruments.

Two lumberjacks enjoy music in the bunkhouse. One dances a jig while the other plays a fiddle.

Primary Source

A Lumberjack Song

Lumberjacks working near Wisconsin's Peshtigo (**pesh** ti goh) Brook liked to sing as a group. Here are some lyrics from "The Peshtigo Brook Song":

> In the woods among the trees
> Humming like a swarm of bees,
> Saws and axes, jingle bells,
> Mixed with shouting, whoops, and yells.
> Some were sawing on a pine,
> And the skidders close behind,
> Some their path in loading took
> Way up on Peshtigo Brook.

Telling Tall Tales

A tall tale is a story that is told in an **exaggerated** (ig **za** juh ray tuhd) way. Some tall tales are based on real people or events. Tall tales can sound true, but they're actually fiction.

Lumberjacks loved telling tall tales around the bunkhouse woodstove in the evenings. Sometimes they had contests to see who could tell the best tall tales. The stories helped them laugh and relax at the end of the day.

The Hodag

The story of the Hodag (**hoh** dag) was a favorite tall tale in logging camps. Experienced lumberjacks often told this story to newcomers. They explained

What Makes a Tall Tale?

These are the elements of a tall tale:
1. The main character is a "larger than life" hero with superhuman abilities. For example, they are very tall, fast, or strong.
2. The main character gets help from an object or an animal.
3. The tale describes an everyday problem. The main character solves the problem in funny ways.
4. The events and actions are usually exaggerated.

exaggerated: described as larger or greater than what is true

Rhinelander, Wisconsin, is known as the "Home of the Hodag." This postcard from Rhinelander shows what a hodag is supposed to look like.

that a Hodag was a fierce animal the size of an alligator. It roamed Wisconsin's Northwoods. This fierce creature had a terrifying scream that could raise the hair on the back of the neck of the bravest new lumberjack.

As one lumberjack was telling the story, sometimes a second lumberjack went outside. The lumberjack outside pretended to be a Hodag. He yelled and growled! The new worker's eyes widened in fear as he listened. Later, the newcomer laughed when he realized the storyteller made it all up!

In 1893, a timber cruiser named Eugene Shepard reported he saw a real Hodag. It happened near the town of Rhinelander, Wisconsin.

Eugene described the vicious beast this way:

> It was a seven-foot-long lizard-like beast. It looked to weigh about 185 pounds. The beast had a large head with two horns growing out on either side of it. It had large fangs and green eyes. The body of the beast was covered with short black hair. Its back was covered with spikes. It had a long tail. The Hodag had four short legs with claws. From its nostril spewed flame and smoke. It smelled terrible, like a skunk.

Shepard drew a sketch of the beast. His drawing was published in the Rhinelander newspaper. People saw the picture and wondered if it was real!

Several lumberjacks went looking for the beast. However, when they found the creature, they quickly saw it was a hoax (**hohks**). The Hodag's body was actually a tree stump covered with an ox hide. The horns and spikes came from oxen and cattle. The hoax fooled thousands of people and brought fame to Rhinelander. Today, you can visit Rhinelander and see a huge statue of a Hodag.

Paul Bunyan

A drawing of Paul Bunyan and Babe the Blue Ox

The story of Paul Bunyan is another tall tale. Paul Bunyan was a giant lumberjack with powerful tree-chopping skills. He was very tall, strong, and clever. Stories of Paul Bunyan often included Babe, his giant blue ox.

Lumberjacks enjoyed stories of Paul Bunyan because they involved logging activities. Many lumberjacks believed (or pretended to believe) Paul Bunyan was a real person.

Here are some famous Paul Bunyan stories:

- Paul Bunyan tied a rope to the end of his axe and cut forty acres of pine trees with a single swing.

- One day, the cook at the logging camp was late blowing the dinner horn. Paul Bunyan burst into the kitchen. He grabbed the dinner horn and pointed it out the window. Then he blew the horn so hard that the noise uprooted 80 acres of pine trees and laid them flat.

- Paul Bunyan had his own cook named Big Joe. Big Joe cooked on a griddle that was so big, you couldn't see across it when the steam was thick. The griddle was greased by boys who skated over it with hams on their feet.

- Paul Bunyan carved out the Great Lakes by dragging an axe behind him. He spilled water, and it formed the Mississippi River!

People still tell stories about Paul Bunyan today. You can travel across the Midwest and find statues of Paul and Babe the Blue Ox.

Sunday Chores

Sunday was a day of chores in the logging camp. Some men repaired equipment. A traveling preacher might visit. Those interested in hearing the preacher's message gathered in the cookhouse.

The crew washed their clothes on Sundays. They heated water in a large kettle set over a fire. Their washtub was usually a wooden barrel that was sawed in half. They put their dirty clothes in the washtub. They washed the clothes with soap and boiling water. Then they hung the clothes to dry.

Most men also shaved on Sunday. However, they did not take baths. Lumberjacks could go all winter without a bath!

Statues of Paul Bunyan and Babe stand near the entrance to the Wisconsin Logging Museum in Eau Claire, Wisconsin. The Paul Bunyan statue is more than 13 feet tall! It was made by a retired firefighter with the help of local high school students.

Workers at a Rice Lake logging camp wash their clothes on a Sunday afternoon.

Chapter 8

The Log Drive

When the winter's work ended, most lumberjacks went home. Others were hired to move logs to the sawmill.

The temperature warmed by late March or early April. Snow melted and flowed into the rivers. The water level rose. The water was ice-cold.

It was time to move the logs to the mill. The logs were huge and heavy. Some logs were up to 16 feet long! Moving the logs was difficult and dangerous.

The River Highway

Moving logs by floating them on a river was called a log drive. The lumberjacks who did this work were called log drivers.

A log drive took a few days or a full month. It depended on how far the cutting site was from the sawmill.

The Log Drive 53

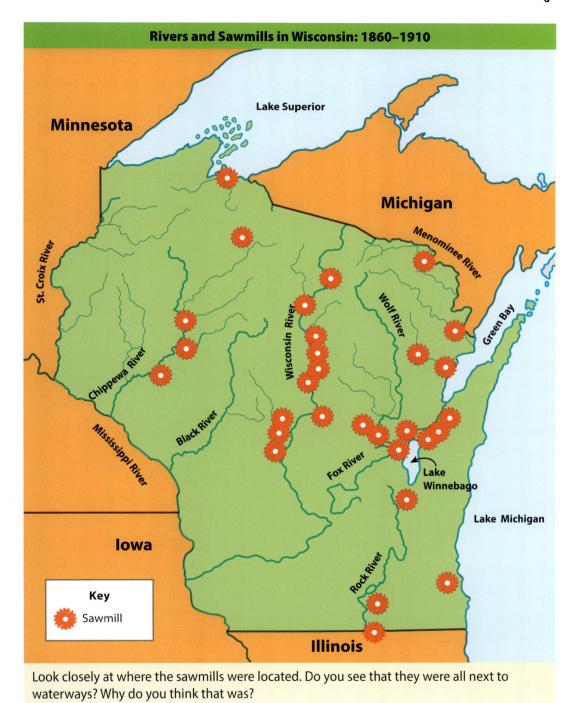

Rivers and Sawmills in Wisconsin: 1860–1910

Look closely at where the sawmills were located. Do you see that they were all next to waterways? Why do you think that was?

Members of a log driving crew near the Chippewa River in about 1905

Log drivers were paid twice as much as regular lumberjacks. They earned more money because the job was so dangerous. Log drivers needed to be incredibly strong. They needed to have good balance. They needed to move quickly and stay calm in stressful situations.

Log driving was wet work. Log drivers needed clothes that dried quickly. They wore light cotton overalls and flannel shirts, often in red and black plaid (**plad**). Some people called this kind of shirt the "uniform of the north."

The Front Crew

Log drivers were divided into two groups: a front crew and a rear crew. The front crew went first. They stood on the logs and steered them in the river. They tried to keep the logs moving forward so they didn't get stuck and block the river.

The front crew traveled with the logs. They often walked or rode on top of the logs! The crew wore boots with sharp spikes on the bottom. The spikes dug into the soft pine logs. These special

Pike pole

A pike pole was a wooden pole with a sharp metal point at one end. It was about 16 feet long. Log drivers used pike poles to balance on top of logs.

How Is a River Like a Highway?

When logging began, no roads stretched across the entire state. Rivers were the easiest way to get from place to place. The river was like a highway for the logs.

In Wisconsin, rivers run in two directions:

1. In northeastern Wisconsin, rivers flow north, toward Lake Winnebago, the Fox River, and then Green Bay. Green Bay is part of Lake Michigan, which is one of the Great Lakes. The Great Lakes are connected to each other by small rivers and streams. The St. Lawrence River runs from the Great Lakes to the Atlantic Ocean. If you drop a feather in the Fox River, it could travel all the way to the Atlantic!
2. In central and northwestern Wisconsin, rivers flow south, toward the Mississippi River. If you drop a feather in the Wisconsin River, it could travel to the Mississippi River. Then it could float all the way to the Gulf of Mexico!

boots helped the crew balance on the slippery, wet logs. When a log driver lost his footing, he tumbled into the ice-cold river. This happened every day. Injuries were common and part of the job.

Log drivers used a tool called a pike pole to keep their balance. They also used pike poles to steer the logs and keep them from getting stuck. They used another tool called a peavey (**pee** vee) to grab, stab, push, roll, or move logs in the river.

The log drivers pushed and prodded the logs to keep them moving forward. At the same time, they kept their balance to avoid falling. They worked like this for ten hours every day!

Peavey

A peavey was a wooden pole with a big hook at one end. It was five or six feet long. Log drivers used the peavey to move logs floating in a river.

A portrait of a log driver holding a peavey

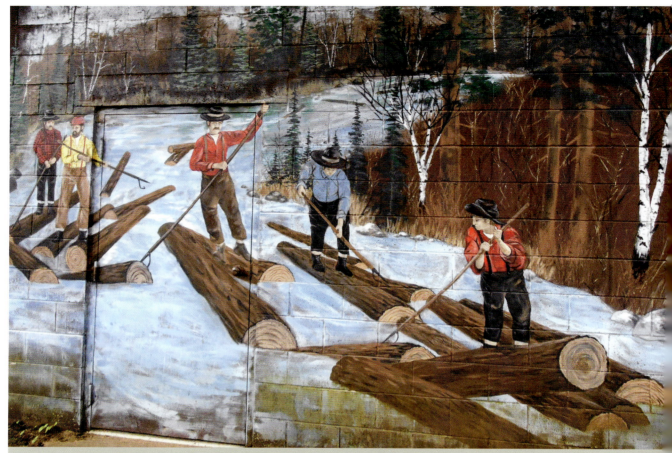

A front crew steers logs in this mural at the Pioneer Park Historical Complex in Rhinelander, Wisconsin.

The Rear Crew

The rear crew followed the front crew. They didn't ride on logs. Instead, they walked next to the river.

Sometimes logs floated away from the front crew. Some logs got stuck in mud or sand. Other logs got tangled in low-hanging tree branches. The rear crew watched out for stray or stuck logs. They waded into the icy water. They used pike poles or peaveys to push the logs back where they belonged.

Sometimes a log floated up onto the riverbank and got stuck on dry land. The logs were too heavy to be pushed back into the water. So the crew used chains to connect the log to a team of horses. The horses pulled the log back into the water.

The Bateau Boat

The rear crew used a boat called a bateau (ba **toh**). The word *bateau* is French. A bateau had a flat bottom. It was about 35 feet long and five feet wide. A bateau was very sturdy. It was hard to tip over. It was the perfect boat for a log drive.

Crews used the bateau to look for logs that were left behind or stuck on rocks. The bateau was handled by an experienced driver. He steered it over rapids and around hazards like boulders and branches.

The log drivers didn't want to lose any of their company's logs. Every log in the river was worth money at the sawmill.

A log driving crew in bateau boats in about 1900

The Night Boom

What kept logs from floating away while the log drivers slept? The crew set up a barrier to keep the logs in one place. The barrier was called a river boom. Sometimes it was called a night boom.

The boom was made by linking several floating logs together. The logs were connected end to end like a chain. The boom acted like a fence across the river. It was held in place by a pile of rocks on the riverbank.

Many logging companies had river drives at the same time. Every night, many booms were built up and down the same rivers.

A Floating Kitchen

A wooden raft followed along behind the log drivers. The raft was called a wanigan (**wo** ni guhn). A wanigan was a floating kitchen. It held a cast-iron cooking stove and the food supply for the crew. This is where the cook and cookee worked.

The wanigan served as the office for the river boss. It also stored the tents, **bedrolls**, and personal belongings of the log drivers. Some logging companies even had floating bunkhouses attached to the wanigan.

At the end of the day, log drivers tied the wanigan to a tree on the shore. This way, it would not float away overnight.

A Long Day's Work

Log drivers woke up as early as 3:00 a.m. They ate breakfast before dawn. They usually ate two lunches a day, one at mid-morning and one about 1:00 p.m. They worked as long as they had daylight and the river logs were moving.

---

bedrolls: bedding that is rolled up for carrying

This wanigan was named the *Dancing Annie* It was used by a lumber company near Eagle Rapids in about 1900.

At the end of each day, they set up a night boom. The crew got their tents and bedrolls from the wanigan. They put up their tents on the river's edge. Then they lined up for supper.

Supper on a log drive might include salt pork, beans, potatoes, biscuits, coffee, and a piece of raisin pie. Salt pork is like bacon, but it is heavily salted so it doesn't spoil.

After supper, the men greased their boots with tallow (**ta** loh). Tallow is animal fat. They rubbed the tallow into the leather to keep their boots waterproof. They filed the spikes on the bottoms of their boots to keep the spikes sharp. Then it was time for bed.

Log drivers worked hard. Sometimes they skipped meals or ate very little. They did not want to stop working. They wanted to avoid a logjam.

Log drivers take a short break to eat lunch. A bateau boat rests on the shore behind them.

Chapter 9

Challenge down the River

Rivers are not all the same. So each log drive was not the same. Rivers don't flow in a straight line. Sometimes the water flows faster or slower. Some rivers are wide and some are narrow. Some are deep and some are shallow. Many rivers have boulders or rocky rapids. All of this made it hard to move logs down the river.

Thousands of huge logs rushed downstream. Log drivers steered the logs away from the sides of the river. Some log drivers were part of the jam crew. Their job was to prevent logjams. A logjam happens when logs get stuck and block the flow of the river. With so many logs on the river, logjams could not always be avoided.

What Caused a Logjam?

A logjam started when logs caught on rocks or branches. The crew moved the jammed logs with their peaveys or pike poles. Then the logs floated on.

However, sometimes the crew could not move the jammed logs out of the way. Other logs floated into the jammed logs. This happened quickly.

The river's **current** moved more logs downstream. The pile of jammed logs got bigger. If the crew could not move the first jammed logs out of the way, other logs smashed into them! All the logs became wedged into each other.

Logjams could be huge. In 1869, a large logjam happened on the Chippewa River. It was 15 miles long. In some places, the logs were piled 30 feet high. Another logjam on the Wolf River was almost 60 feet high!

A logjam was a log driver's nightmare. Logjams delayed the logs' arrival at the mill for days or weeks. A large jam often blocked the flow of the river itself. The logs created a **dam** in the river. This caused the water to back up. The water level rose behind the jam. The rising water lifted up the incoming logs and put them on top of the jam.

Even small logjams were a problem. The river water had to flow around the logjam. The water could wash out the riverbank. Sometimes it flooded the shore.

---

current: part of a body of water that moves in a certain direction

dam: a barrier that holds back the flow of water

A man sits in the middle of a logjam near Black River Falls, Wisconsin. Do you see him? The logjam was so big, the man is almost hard to spot!

How Did They Break Up the Jam?

The jam crew walked on top of the pile of jammed logs. They used their tools to get the logs to move.

Large logjams were harder to break up. Sometimes the crew had to use horses. They tied the horses to the logs with rope. Then the horses pulled the logs free. When a logjam broke up, the crew had to move out of the way quickly and jump to safety.

Some companies used dynamite to blow up large logjams. This was dangerous for the crew and animals. Some logs were damaged and could not be used at the sawmill. This cost the company money.

Breaking up a big logjam could take many weeks. Sometimes hundreds of men and horses were involved. A huge logjam happened on the St. Croix River in 1886. It took 200 men, 100 horses, and two steamboats to break it up!

Sluicing Logs through the Dam

Dams were built along some rivers to control the flow of water. Early dams often were made of wood or rock. A gate in the dam could be opened or closed to control how much water was able to flow.

When log drivers reached a dam, they used a boom to hold the logs back. When everyone was ready, they opened the gate. Then the log drivers stood on the dam and sluiced (**sloost**), or directed, each log through the dam. They used pike poles or peaveys to control the logs as they moved through the rushing water. This was dangerous work. The crew needed to think quickly and keep their balance.

Challenge down the River 65

Primary Source

Postcard from a Logjam

A logjam was big news for people who lived near the river. Crowds of families from surrounding towns and farms came to watch the jam crew work.

A photographer took this photo of a logjam on the Chippewa River. He made the photo into a postcard. This photo was colorized before it was turned into a postcard. That means it was colored by hand with crayon or oil paint.

The Wisconsin River

The Wisconsin River is about 430 miles long. It starts in northern Wisconsin and flows south across the entire state. It joins the Mississippi River in the southwestern corner of the state. You can see the path of the Wisconsin River on the map on page 53.

The Wisconsin River begins as a small, winding stream. Farther south, the river widens. It has many tight turns, rushing rapids, and waterfalls. The current can be very fast. This made log driving extremely difficult. It was almost impossible for river drivers to safely move logs over large rapids and waterfalls.

The largest logjam in Wisconsin history happened on the Wisconsin River in 1884. Grandfather Falls is a long stretch of heavy rapids north of Merrill. It is the highest waterfall on the Wisconsin River. It is almost one mile long and drops almost 90 feet. In the logjam at Grandfather Falls, 80 million board feet of lumber were backed up for miles. Workers tried to clear the jam for more than a month, but they couldn't do it. Finally, they used dynamite to break up the jam and send the logs on their way.

Lumber Rafting

It was too hard to float logs on parts of the Wisconsin River. Instead, the crew used huge rafts to carry the logs. One raft could carry a big pile of logs.

The crew made each raft by tying many logs together:
- First they used a tool called an auger (**aw** gur) to drill holes in the ends of several logs.
- Next, they put big iron pins in the holes.
- Then they put the logs next to each other. They wrapped rope or chain around the iron pins to tie the logs together.

By the 1850s, log drivers were using about 3,000 lumber rafts on the Wisconsin River. These rafts moved more than one million board feet of lumber every year. The rafts were piloted by men who rode on top of each raft.

Auger

This picture shows lumber rafts on the Wisconsin River in 1886. The picture was taken by a photographer named H.H. Bennett. In the 1880s, Bennett used his camera to document the lives of river raft pilots. His photographs became famous. Today his work can be seen at the H.H. Bennett Studio historic site in Wisconsin Dells, Wisconsin.

Some parts of the Wisconsin River were dangerous for rafts. A raft would be smashed into splinters if it got caught in boulders or rough rapids.

The Wisconsin River flows through narrow bluffs at the Dells. When the crew arrived at the bluffs, they stopped. They took the rafts apart into smaller pieces. Then they rode through the narrow section of the river on the smaller pieces. Afterward they put the rafts back together and continued on to the sawmill.

Primary Source

Life as a Raftsman

Ceylon Childs Lincoln was a lumber raftsman. In 1868, he rafted down the Wisconsin River for the first time. This is how he described what it was like to go over a dam:

> The ice went out on the river April 17, and the next day we started with five men at each oar, to run [go through] the Stevens Point dam. We ran down the center of the river, until we reached the dam. The current ran between two piers, about thirty feet apart; between these piers was the slide, constructed of long logs (called "fingers") fastened with chains to the dam; on either side of the slide, the water dropped about fifteen feet. Below the dam, the river boiled and rolled into whitecaps. If one was fortunate enough to make the slide properly, he could make his landing in the right place; otherwise there was great danger of saddle bagging [getting caught on] one of the piers and breaking it to pieces. Sometimes, the raft turned a compete somersault. . . . Even when going down the slide, the raft generally sank until we were standing in waist deep in the water. We seldom had a chance to go to the raft on

which the cook shanty was placed for our meals. Our food was brought [to us] . . . by a small skiff [a small boat]. The food was very good. We never floated down at night, but each raft tied up, with a half-inch cable to the [river] bank. When our fleet arrived at the mouth of the [Mississippi] River there was great rejoicing, as the hard work was mostly over. The nine Wisconsin rafts were coupled into one large Mississippi raft, with a cook shanty in the middle, and long table where men could be seated for meals. Our Mississippi River Raft consisted of three Wisconsin rafts [across] and three deep, making a raft 144 feet wide and 380 long.

After reading:

What does Ceylon's letter tell you about what log driving was like?

What questions would you like to ask Ceylon?

Ceylon does not include details about how he felt about this work. Put yourself in his shoes. How would you feel?

How is this job different from being a lumberjack in the woods? How is it similar?

Chapter 10

From Logs to Lumber

After many days or weeks on the river, the logs finally reached the sawmill. The river drivers' work was over. The work at the sawmill began.

Workers line up the logs at a sawmill on the Wisconsin River. Next, they will push the logs up the ramp and into the building. This picture was taken in Wisconsin Rapids in 1930.

The Mill Pond

First, the logs went to the mill pond. The pond was made by a dam on the river. This is where logs were sorted.

Many logging companies moved logs down the river at the same time. Logs often arrived at the mill in a jumble. Logs from one company were mixed up with logs from another. Logging companies were paid based on the number of logs they delivered to the mill. So it was important to know which logs belonged to which company.

Back at the logging camp, a mark was stamped on the end of each log. At the mill pond, sawmill workers used the marks to sort the logs.

Working in the Sawmill

A sawmill was a loud and busy place. A typical sawmill building was one or two stories tall. Workers hauled and measured lumber. The saw screeched as it cut wood. The smell of sawdust filled the air.

Often, men and boys from the same family worked at the mill together. Most sawmill workers did more than one job. Many people worked together to turn the logs into lumber.

Foreman

The foreman ran the mill and was in charge of the workers.

Millwright

The millwright (**mil** rIt) designed and built the mill. He knew how each part worked. The millwright took care of the building and the machines. He fixed anything that broke.

Saw Filer

The saw filer sharpened the saw blades so the mill could cut as much wood as possible.

Sawyer

A sawyer is anyone who saws trees and cuts them into logs. At the mill, the sawyer controlled the machines that sawed logs into lumber. Sawyers did many jobs at the mill. They knew how to use many different saws and equipment.

Scaler

The scaler checked the quality of the logs. He measured each log. He wrote down the number of board feet in his logbook. A scaler at the logging camp scaled the logs after they were cut. A second scaler checked logs at the mill.

Steps in the Sawmill Process

After the logs were sorted by company mark, they were ready for the sawmill. First, the logs were debarked (dee **bahrkt**). This means the bark was removed. Next, the logs were cut into boards with a **mechanical** (mi **ka** ni kuhl) saw. Then an edging saw smoothed the rough edges of the boards.

The last step was called planing. To plane something means to make it smooth or even. A planer machine trimmed each board to an even thickness and width.

Finally, the boards were ready to be sold! Smaller mills sold lumber to people who lived nearby. People came to the lumberyard to buy the lumber. They used a horse-pulled wagon to haul it home.

---

mechanical: made or operated by a machine

Larger mills made more lumber than they could sell locally. The extra lumber was sold to places farther away. Sometimes the lumber was transported by ship down the Mississippi River.

The Waterwheel

Sawmills were built near rivers for another important reason. Fast-moving water is a source of energy. Early mills used waterwheels to capture energy from the river's current. They used that energy to power the saws!

A waterwheel was a huge wheel made of wood. Often, the waterwheel was built against the side of the sawmill building, at the edge of the river.

The rim of the waterwheel was lined with paddles. Water from the river flowed over the waterwheel. The force of the water pushed against the wooden paddles. This made the wheel spin.

As the giant wheel turned, it powered smaller wheels inside the building. These smaller wheels were connected to a wooden rod that moved the mechanical saw.

Waterwheels only worked when enough water was flowing quickly. If a stream dried up, the mill closed. When a river froze in the winter, the wheel did not turn.

Water power!
Waterwheels used the power of water to do things that people or animals could not easily do. They were used to: grind grain into flour; grind wood into pulp to make paper; and turn wool fiber into cloth.

A waterwheel on the side of a mill

> **Dangers of the Sawmill**
>
> Working at a sawmill was not an easy job. People got hurt. For example, workers got hit in the head with heavy lumber.
>
> The most dangerous part of the sawmill was the saw itself. In the early days, sawmills did not have rules to keep workers safe. Workers did not cover their ears to protect them from the noise. They did not wear safety glasses. Sometimes a worker's hand got caught in the saw and they lost fingers.

Water Turbine-Powered Mill

For many years, sawmills depended on wooden waterwheels. After about 1850, most mills switched from wooden waterwheels to metal turbines (**tur** binz).

A turbine is a circular machine with metal blades. Turbines work under the water. The water current made the turbine spin. This powered the gears that moved the saw up and down.

A turbine was easier to take care of than a waterwheel. A turbine did not freeze up in the winter. It did not need to be built by the millwright like a waterwheel. Instead, a turbine was built in a machine shop and sent to the mill.

By the middle of the 1900s, most mills stopped using water power. Instead, their saws were powered by electric motors.

Types of Saws

Pit Saw

The earliest saws were pit saws. Pit saws were six to eight feet long. They had handles at each end. This is how they worked:
- A pit was dug in the ground.
- A log was laid across the pit.
- One worker was in the pit, underneath the log. He was called the pitman. Another worker was above ground. He was called the top sawyer.
- Each worker held one end of a saw. They moved the saw up and down to cut the log. In a good day, they could saw 100 to 200 feet of lumber.

Sash Saw

The sash saw was the first saw powered by water. Sometimes the sash saw was called an up-and-down saw because it moved up and down like a pit saw. However, a sash saw was moved by a waterwheel, not by people.

Muley Saw

After 1830, sawmills began using muley (**myoo** lee) saws. The muley saw was lighter and faster than the sash saw. It needed less power to work. Its cuts were more accurate. However, the muley saw made a lot of sawdust. And it only cut when the saw was moving down. The saw had to move back up before it could cut again.

An illustration of an up-and-down sawmill. A waterwheel turned a crank that moved the saw.

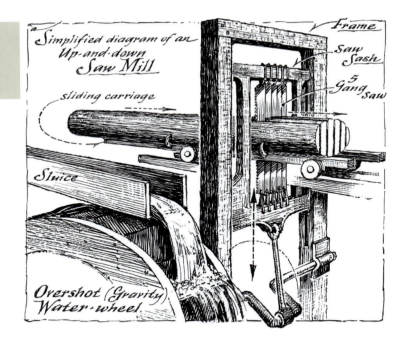

Circular Saw

By the 1850s, the circular saw replaced the muley saw. A circular saw has a round blade. The blade spun around and cut through the log. It did not need to be moved up or down. A circular saw was fast. It could cut ten times more lumber than a muley saw. However, it created huge piles of sawdust. Sawdust is very **flammable**. A spark from a machine could land on the sawdust and start a fire.

Gang Saw

One answer to the sawdust problem was the gang saw. A gang saw had many blades that were arranged in rows. These

flammable: easy to catch on fire

Two men use a circular saw to cut a log. A man stands at either end. They work together to guide the log across the saw.

blades could cut 20 or more boards at a single time. The blades were thin and sharp. They made narrow cuts and created less sawdust.

Some mills used a circular saw to cut a large log into smaller pieces. Then they used gang saws to cut those pieces into boards.

Band Saw

Another answer to the sawdust problem was the band saw. The band saw was a large band of steel. It was about 15 inches wide and 50 feet long. The ends were connected, like a giant rubber band. The steel band passed over wheels that moved to operate the saw.

By the 1890s, all the large mills used band saws. The band saw made narrow cuts in the wood. This created less sawdust and helped save lumber.

This drawing of a band saw from 1907 was part of an advertisement in a newspaper called *The Canada Lumberman and Woodworker*. The ad encouraged mill owners to reduce waste by replacing their circular saws with band saws.

Sawdust Towns

Sawmills were built all over central and northern Wisconsin. Families soon moved to the area where a sawmill was built. As more people arrived, villages began to form. Many towns and cities in Wisconsin began because of the logging **industry**.

They were nicknamed "sawdust" towns because people depended on the sawmills for jobs.

Sawmills were built near rivers. Some of those rivers were: the Black, Chippewa, Fox, Rock, St. Croix, Wolf, and Wisconsin. (See the map on page page 53!)

The town of Oshkosh is near the Fox River. In 1852, there were three sawmills in Oshkosh. By the late 1800s, Oshkosh had many more sawmills. It also had many businesses that made things out of wood.

industry: a type of business

From Logs to Lumber   79

Spring was a very busy time of year in sawmill towns. Lumberjacks returned home with money in their pockets. People gathered for parties and dances. Many sawmill towns had their own baseball teams. People came together to watch them play. And log rolling contests drew crowds from all around.

Log Rolling

At the end of the log drives, lumberjacks competed in log rolling contests. Two lumberjacks balanced on the same log floating on the water. They tried to make each other fall off the log. First they ran in place to make the log spin. Then they stopped abruptly. The person who kept their balance was the winner.

Today, log rolling has become a serious athletic event. Men, women, and even kids compete in the sport. They log roll in lakes, pools, and ponds all over the United States and Canada. The Lumberjack World Championships happen every year in Hayward, Wisconsin.

Two boys compete in a log rolling contest on Lake Wingra in Madison, Wisconsin.

Chapter 11

The Power of Steam

By the 1890s, people were using lumber as fast as logging crews and sawmills could produce it. Many of the pine forests in Wisconsin had been cut down. Logging companies looked for ways to produce more lumber in less expensive ways. And mill owners wanted to find new types of wood to turn into lumber.

New tools were available to help them. These tools were powered by steam. Every part of logging changed with the use of steam power.

What Is a Steam Engine?

Steam engines use energy from steam to make machines move or work:

- A steam engine burns fuel to make a fire.
- The fire boils water and makes steam.

- The steam creates pressure that moves a piston. A piston is piece of metal that can move up and down.
- The piston is attached to another part of the machine. When the piston moves, the other part moves, too. This movement makes the machine work.

Steam engines can turn wheels, operate saws, power boats, and do other kinds of work.

Steam Power on the River

Logging companies began using steam power on large rivers like the Mississippi. They used steamboats to push rafts of logs. Log drivers no longer needed to float logs on a river.

People traveled on steamboats, too. In the mid- and late 1800s, steamboats were the main way people and things traveled. This changed when railroads were built.

This postcard shows a steamboat towing a huge raft of lumber on the Mississippi River.

Steam-Powered Trains

Early trains ran on steam. Steam engines moved the wheels of the **locomotive** (**loh** kuh **moh** tiv). Steam and smoke were released through a chimney on top of the engine. When steam passed through the chimney, the train made a *chuff* sound.

The US government still owned land in Wisconsin. In the 1860s and 1870s, the government gave land to the railroads. Over time, railroad companies began building tracks to be used for logging.

Logs could be moved by train. Logging companies often built their own tracks into a forest. When there were no more trees to cut, the company pulled up the tracks. They moved the tracks to a new part of the forest.

locomotive: an engine that moves by its own power

Steam-powered logging trains

Railroads allowed loggers to cut timber far away from rivers and streams. Logging camps no longer needed to be near water. Lumberjacks no longer needed to stack logs on the riverbank and wait for spring. Now, they could cut and move timber all year long.

Railroads also made it easier to work in remote parts of the forest. Trains could haul food, equipment, lumberjacks, and animals to camps deep in the woods.

Railroads did not replace dangerous log drives for everyone. Log driving cost less money than moving logs by train. Smaller companies could not afford to use the railroads. Floating logs to the sawmills continued into the 1900s.

Train or locomotive?
Do you know the difference? A train is a series of train cars that move on a track. A locomotive is the engine that powers the train. It can be at the front or back. A locomotive at the front pulls the train down the track. A locomotive at the back pushes the train forward.

Logging Hardwood Forests

Railroads did not only change *where* logging happened. Railroads also changed *what kind* of trees were cut down.

Trees are either softwood or hardwood. Softwood trees grow quickly. They are light. They can float. White pines are one kind of softwood tree.

Hardwood trees grow slowly. They are heavy. They cannot float. Maple, oak, birch, and elm trees are examples of hardwood trees.

Loggers had ignored hardwood trees for years. Huge forests of hardwood trees still stood, even after most pine trees were cut down.

Hardwoods were easy to haul on rail cars. By the early 1870s, logging companies were cutting hardwood trees such as maple and oak.

Clear-Cutting

Before railroads, loggers only cut trees that could float. They cut the pines and left the other trees in the forest.

Railroads gave logging companies a way to move hardwood trees. Now, all the trees in a forest were cut down. This is called clear-cutting. Logging companies knew sawmills wanted many kinds of trees. Different trees produced different kinds of lumber.

> **Did you know?** Hardwood lumber is used to make furniture, flooring, and musical instruments.

Steam-Powered Log Hauler

As railroads made their way north in Wisconsin, a new machine began appearing in logging camps. The huge machine was called a log hauler. It was powered by a wood-burning steam engine.

A steam log hauler transports logs from a logging camp near Rice Lake, Wisconsin, in 1914.

The Power of Steam 85

A log hauler looked a little like a train locomotive. Three workers operated it. The steersman sat at the front. He used a steering wheel to keep the machine going in the right direction. The train engineer sat in the cab behind the boiler. He kept the machine running. The fireman made sure the boiler had enough fuel.

The log hauler could pull a sled loaded with logs out of the woods. Then the logs were loaded onto a train and taken to the sawmill. Log haulers could pull many more logs than a team of horses. Oxen and horses were no longer needed.

Steam-Powered Sawmills

By the 1850s, sawmills began to use steam power, too. Many sawmills used steam engines instead of waterwheels or turbines.

Trains soon became the easiest way for people to travel, too. Here, people get ready to board a steam-powered train in Green Bay, Wisconsin, in about 1901.

A steam engine could power the sawblade. Sawmills no longer needed to be built on riverbanks.

Not all sawmill owners switched to steam power. Steam power was expensive. A steam engine cost more money to build than a waterwheel. Steam engines needed coal.

Most sawmills that used steam power were bigger. They were built in larger cities like Fond du Lac, Oshkosh, Eau Claire, and La Crosse. Many smaller sawmills kept using water power, in places like Peshtigo, Oconto Falls, and Chippewa Falls.

By the 1860s, a **revolution** (re vuh **loo** shuhn) in sawmill technology was taking place. New machines were being invented, such as a mechanical log turner and a machine that moved logs back and forth past a saw. These machines used steam power. They helped sawmills make more lumber with less waste.

Steam Power Changes the Lumber Industry

Steam power changed every part of the logging industry. Steam power meant lumberjacks cut logs all year round, not only in winter. Now, sleds full of logs were pulled by steam-powered log haulers and loaded onto trains. Logging sleds were no longer pulled by oxen or horses.

Steam power made it safer and faster to move logs to the sawmill, first with steamboats and then with trains. They could move logs all year long.

Steam power changed sawmills, too. Now they could be located almost anywhere. Steam-powered saws changed how the mills made lumber.

revolution: a big shift or change

The Power of Steam 87

Logging companies were turning trees into lumber as fast as they could. More logging camps moved in. More sawmills opened. In the woods, the sounds of axes and falling trees continued to fill the air.

Primary Source

Memory of a Log Hauler

A manager of a logging company described the log hauler this way:

> The log hauler owned by our company, which is a Phoenix (**fee** niks), was purchased in December 1907 at a cost of $6,000. We have used this steam horse [engine] for four winters, and during that time it has lost only one day, due to one of the parts breaking, which was quickly replaced by the company that made it. Excepting this misfortune, the machine in question has missed but one trip in carrying out its regular schedule.

After Reading:

Did you notice that the writer calls the log hauler a "steam horse"? Why?

How do you think this machine changed the work in the logging camp?

This is what the Cutover looked like in about 1939.

Chapter 12

The Dangers of Cutover Land

Logging companies moved from one part of a forest to another. They left behind bare land and tree stumps. Workers also left behind branches that were too small to be used for lumber. This leftover material was called slash.

By the 1910s, many forests were gone. Acres of tree stumps and slash covered the land where forests once stood. The land looked empty. This bleak landscape came to be known as the Cutover (**kuht** oh vur).

Lumberjacks stand on top of huge logs. The logs are piled on a sled. Behind them, tree stumps cover the land.

Increase Lapham

Increase Lapham

A man named Increase Lapham (**lap** uhm) moved to Wisconsin in 1836. Lapham lived in Milwaukee. He was a scientist. He was very interested in nature. He wrote a book about the plants and shells found near the shore of Lake Michigan.

Increase Lapham saw what was happening in the forests. He saw that acres of trees were being cut.

In 1854, Lapham wrote a book about the importance of forests. Lapham wanted people to understand what was happening to the trees. He wanted people to know why forests were important.

Lapham warned people to stop clear-cutting the forests. He knew that when an entire forest was cut down, it **permanently** changed the land. Lapham warned the state **legislature** (**lej** uh slay chur) to protect the forests. He knew the balance of nature was at risk if there were no more trees. However, few people listened to Lapham's warnings.

Peak Logging Years

The years 1870 to the 1890s were **peak** (**peek**) logging years in Wisconsin. This is when logging companies cut down the most trees. Logging was big business. The people who owned logging companies made a lot of money.

During this time, more and more people moved to the Midwest. As the population grew, so did the need for houses, railroad lines, stores, tools, and other products made from wood. People needed wood, and Wisconsin could provide it. Railroads easily moved lumber from Wisconsin to other states and cities. All kinds of lumber were needed.

Some lawmakers were also part of the logging industry. They owned sawmills. They were more interested in making money than protecting the trees. It seemed like nothing was going to stop logging in the Northwoods.

During the peak logging years, most people did not care how logging changed the forests. Some logging company owners moved to the Midwest from states in the east, such as Maine. Many forests in the east were already cut down. Logging company owners knew Wisconsin's forests would not last forever. However, they continued to cut down trees.

permanently: not brief or temporary
legislature: a group of people who make laws
peak: the highest or busiest point

92 🌲 **Timber!**

This land was destroyed by logging and fire. On the right side of the picture you can see where soil erosion has begun.

The Dangers of Cutover Land 93

The Peshtigo Fire

The town of Peshtigo is located near the western shore of Green Bay. The Peshtigo River flows through town and drains into the bay.

In the summer of 1871, Peshtigo was busy. The town had many sawmills. Many nearby forests were cut down. The Cutover land was covered in dry slash and stumps.

That year, there was a **drought** (**drout**). The spring, summer, and early fall were extremely dry, with very little rain.

A railroad company was building a new railway from Green Bay to Michigan. Just outside of Peshtigo, workers were clearing the land for railroad tracks. They burned the slash and stumps in a brush fire.

On Sunday, October 8, strong winds blew across the dry land. The wind caused the fire to spread. The fire moved quickly. It turned into a raging **inferno** (in **fur** noh) that could not be stopped.

This painting shows a family escaping the fire. Many people fled to nearby fields or jumped into the river.

drought: a period of time with very little rain

inferno: a fire that cannot be stopped

94 Timber!

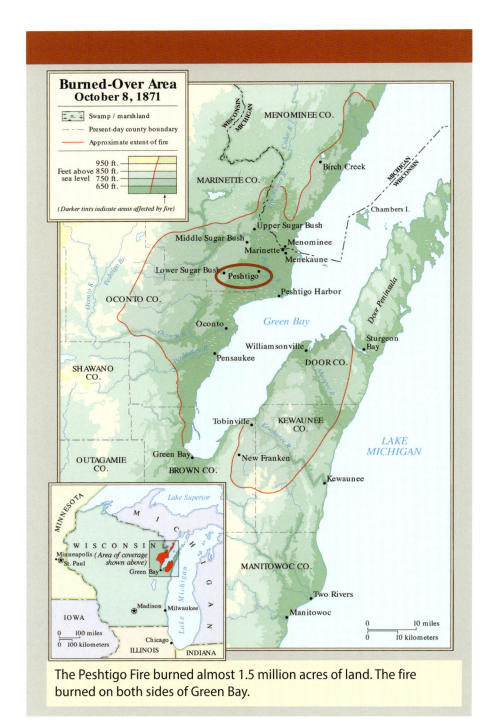

The Peshtigo Fire burned almost 1.5 million acres of land. The fire burned on both sides of Green Bay.

The Dangers of Cutover Land

In just a few minutes, the entire town of Peshtigo was in flames. The fire was so horrific (hoh **ri** fik) that some people thought the world was ending.

The fire burned more than 1 million acres of forest. The fire spread to other towns. The damage in Peshtigo was the worst.

Hours after the fire started, rain began to fall. The rain finally put out the fire. More than 1,000 people died in the fire.

It took many days for help to arrive in Peshtigo. Fire officials in Wisconsin were busy responding to a fire in Chicago that happened on the same day. Both fires happened because of dry weather and drought.

The Great Chicago Fire was one reason for Wisconsin's peak logging years. The fire burned down many of Chicago's buildings. The city needed a lot of board lumber from Wisconsin to rebuild.

In Peshtigo, food and supplies eventually were brought in to help the survivors. People began rebuilding their farms and houses. Peshtigo's sawmill was rebuilt and logging crews started working again. Year by year, the Cutover land got bigger.

What Happened to the Forest?

Logging companies cut millions of acres of forest land. Cutting so many trees changed the forest in many ways. The forest ecosystem (**ee** koh si stuhm) was thrown out of balance. Animals that once lived in the forest died or moved.

What is an ecosystem?
An ecosystem is a community of living things and their environment. Members of an ecosystem depend on one another to survive.

Cutover land was dangerous. Clear-cutting led to erosion (i **roh** zhen) and fires. Erosion happens when soil is slowly taken away by water or wind. Tree roots keep the soil in place. This protects the ground from erosion.

When trees were cut down, their roots decayed. The soil was no longer protected from erosion. Rainstorms could wash the soil away.

The top layer of soil is called topsoil. Topsoil is very important. This is where many plants get their nutrients. When trees were clear-cut, wind blew away the topsoil.

Trees also help keep moisture in the soil. Without trees, the Cutover land became very dry. Stumps and slash were left behind. They could easily catch on fire. Large fires could spread and burn the entire region.

Problems at the Sawmills

Sawmills created problems, too. Sawing logs created a lot of waste, such as sawdust and slab wood. Slab wood is the bark edge of a log. People thought slab wood was useless.

Mills had big piles of slab wood and sawdust. A spark from a machine or saw could land on a pile and start a fire. Raging fires spread quickly.

Mills got rid of their waste by dumping it into rivers. This created islands of trash floating in some rivers.

Working to Solve the Problem

As more forests were clear-cut, the fire danger got worse. Waste from the sawmills piled up. Thousands of acres of dry Cutover land were abandoned. The waste and dry land meant fires would keep happening.

In the late 1800s, Wisconsin lawmakers finally began to do something about this problem.

In 1897, state lawmakers wanted to know how much land had been pineland in central and northern Wisconsin. They also wanted to know who owned the land. They asked a man named Filbert Roth to find out. Roth was a forest expert for the US government.

Roth surveyed the owners of 18.5 million acres in northern Wisconsin. This is what he found:
- 13% of the land was owned by the US government, Wisconsin state government, railroad companies, or Native nations.
- 24% of the land was owned by settlers.
- 63% of the land was owned by logging companies.

Before logging, Roth estimated that northern Wisconsin had about 130 billion feet of pine trees. He discovered that 87% of these pine trees had been cut down! His work proved that the forests full of pine and hardwood trees were gone.

The forest land was now a wasteland. Roth told lawmakers they should protect the rest of the forest lands from logging. He wanted people to plant trees on lands where forests used to be.

Still, No One Listened

Increase Lapham warned people about the dangers of clear-cutting the forests. Many years later, Filbert Roth urged the government to take action and protect the forests. Still, most people did not listen to these warnings. From 1899 to 1904, Wisconsin was the country's top producer of lumber.

98 Timber!

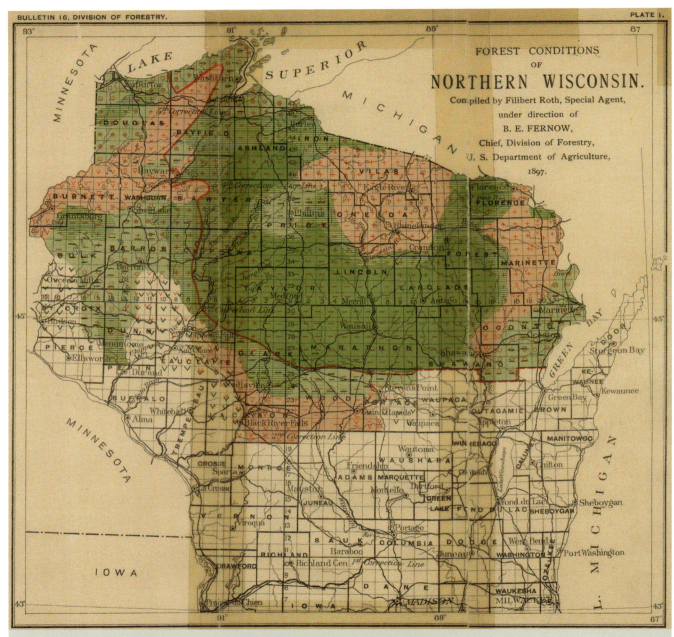

Filbert Roth made this map based on his findings. The map shows where forests were growing in northern Wisconsin in 1897. The pink areas ( ) are pine forests. The green areas ( ) are forests with a mix of pine and hardwood trees. The pink and green areas marked with a dashed red line ( ) show Cutover land.

People still needed lumber for homes, furniture, and tools. People working in the lumber industry still needed jobs. Logging companies continued cutting every pine and hardwood tree.

Logging was a business. One person or family sometimes owned all parts of a logging business, from the cutting site to the sawmill. Owners wanted to produce lumber and make a profit. They wanted workers to cut as many trees as possible, without extra costs.

Most logging company owners did not take care of the land when the work was done. They did not want to pay workers to clean up the slash. They left behind a mess of tangled limbs, stumps, and treetops. Then they moved to other places to cut more trees.

Lumber Industry Decline

Around 1915, a great quiet came over the Northwoods. There were no sounds of axes or crosscut saws. There were no shouts of "Timber!" as another giant pine crashed to the ground. There were no saws slicing through logs and turning them into lumber at sawmills.

In the spring, the ice thawed on the streams and rivers. All you could hear was the murmuring of water running over rapids. There were no log drivers yelling to one another as they steered the logs down the river.

The great pinery was no more. What remained were ghosts of what had been. Thousands of acres of stumps covered northern Wisconsin.

Most logging company owners left Wisconsin. They took their money and jobs to other places. They found new areas where there were trees to cut and money to be made.

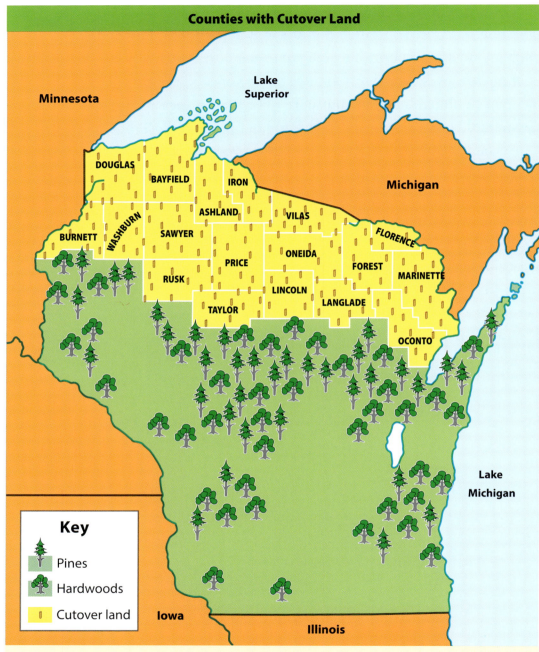

The Cutover covered large parts of 18 counties. Which counties were they? Have you been to this part of the state? What does it look like now?

Many towns and cities grew while the logging industry was booming. The local **economy** (i **kah** nuh mee) depended on logging and lumber. Logging companies employed a lot of people. Many other businesses made and sold wood products like roofing shingles and furniture. In many towns, logging companies built schools, hospitals, and houses for workers.

When the logging era ended, people moved away. Businesses closed. Sawmills were forced to shut down. Many people lost their jobs.

Without logging, many towns and cities needed new ways to keep their economy strong. Some cities began making paper products instead of lumber. Mills needed large trees to make lumber. But they could use smaller trees to make paper. Some areas attracted tourists. Other areas tried to convince people to move to the Cutover and farm the land.

economy: the goods, services, and money that are made and used by a group of people

Chapter 13

Restoring the Land

It took many years for trees to grow big enough to be cut for board lumber. Logging company owners did not want to keep their land and wait for new trees to grow. Instead, they purchased new forest land farther away.

Logging companies were eager to sell their Cutover land. They wanted other people to move in and clean it up. They advertised their northern lands for sale.

Farmers Move to the Cutover

Some people thought the abandoned Cutover would be good for farming. In 1896, the University of Wisconsin published a handbook about farming on the Cutover. This short book showed photos of successful farm families with their crops. There were pictures of healthy farm animals, such as cattle, sheep, horses, and goats.

Restoring the Land 103

Primary Source

Postcard

Postcards like this one were a kind of advertisement. They were used to **persuade** (pur **swayd**) farmers to move to the Cutover. This card shows a picture of Julius Koehler outside of his home with two other people. They are holding enormous vegetables. This is printed under the picture: "The vegetables show what can be raised on our lightest soil."

The home of Julius Koehler, Secretary of our Board. His barns are to the left and not shown in this view. The vegetables show what can be raised on our lightest soil.

However, pictures like this one were exaggerated. Sometimes the photographers **manipulated** (muh **ni** pyuh **lay** ted) the photos to change how they looked.

persuade: to win over to a belief or way of acting

manipulated: changed in a way that is untrue

After reading:

What is your opinion of the people who created pictures like this one?

Do you think most people believed these photos were true? Why or why not?

This picture made farming look easier than it really was. How do you think that made people feel?

How do people manipulate photos today? Why do you think they do this?

What clues can you look for to see if a photo has been manipulated?

The handbook was a type of advertisement. It was designed to convince people to buy Cutover land and use it for farming. Some of the photos were staged. This means the pictures were not true or real.

The handbook was given to people all over Europe and Canada. It was even translated into German and Norwegian. Immigrants wanted to move to the United States. Many immigrants dreamed of owning land. The trees, lakes, and landscape of Wisconsin reminded them of their homelands.

By the 1920s, thousands of immigrants moved to the Cutover to farm.

Stump Removal

Many people were convinced to move to the Cutover. When they arrived, the land did not look the way the handbook and postcards had promised. The fields were rocky. They were covered with tree stumps and slash. The new owners needed to clear the land before planting crops.

One of the first things to do was remove the stumps. The stumps were enormous. They could be four feet tall. Sometimes they were more than four feet wide. Removing the giant stumps wasn't easy. Some farmers left the stumps in the fields and simply plowed around them.

A giant tree stump is being pulled from the ground.

This is what a stump looked like as it was exploding!

Some farmers used machines called stump pullers to remove the stumps. Other farmers used dynamite to blow up the stumps. Dynamite was faster, but people often got hurt.

By 1922, settlers in the Cutover cleared stumps from more than 130,000 acres of land.

Farming on the Cutover

Farmers spent a lot of time and money to turn Cutover land into farmland. However, the land wasn't very good for farming.

The soil was too sandy. The ground was full of rocks. Farmers had to pick up the rocks or plow around them. Some rocks were too big to move.

Many crops didn't have enough time to grow. A growing season is measured by the number of days without any frost. The growing season in northern Wisconsin was about 119 days long. But crops like corn needed more than 119 days to grow and ripen. The growing season in southern Wisconsin was about 38 days longer. Crops in southern Wisconsin had enough time to grow.

Farmers on the Cutover did their best to get by. Some farmers raised animals and grew enough food for their own family to eat. They traded eggs and extra food in town for things they needed, such as flour or sugar. However, many farms were far away from town. This made it hard to get crops to market.

People began to realize it was a mistake to use Cutover land for farming. The soil and climate in northern Wisconsin were best for growing trees. Some farmers stayed on their farms, but many did not. Many gave up trying to farm on the Cutover lands.

The Cutover Problem

Farming was not the answer to the problem of the Cutover. Some people thought the Cutover would repair itself. They thought the trees would grow back on their own. Over time, people realized this was wrong.

Without trees, there was nothing to keep heavy rains from tearing at the soil. Huge gullies formed. A gully is a large trench cut into the land by fast-moving water. Slash still covered much of the Cutover. Fire continued to be a threat.

Restoring the Land 107

The Cutover was bare, burned, and dry. The land was not going to recover on its own.

A Forestry Law

Some people believed the forests needed protection. In 1903, state lawmakers passed a forestry law.

The new law did many things to help the Cutover lands. For example, the law created:
- A state department of forestry
- A system of state forests
- A **forest reserve**, including 62,000 acres of land in Forest, Oneida, Vilas, and Iron Counties
- A new job to oversee the work of protecting forest land. This job was called the state forester.

What is forestry?
Forestry is the science of growing and caring for trees in forests. Forestry involves caring for forests in ways that benefit humans and the environment.

Wisconsin's First State Forester

In 1904, Wisconsin got 20,000 acres of vacant land from the US government. The state wanted to use the land to create new forests.

That same year, Wisconsin hired its first state forester. His name was Edward Merriam Griffith. Griffith was worried that people would continue cutting and destroying the forests. He wanted people to learn about the benefits of reforestation (ree **for** uh **stay** shuhn). Griffith started forest reserves. These forests were owned by the state. They were protected. The trees would not be harmed or cut down.

Griffith taught people how to prevent forest fires. He hired fire wardens. A fire warden enforces fire safety laws.

A forester is a person who practices forestry and manages forest lands.

forest reserve: area of forest protected by the government in which trees cannot be cut down for profit

Griffith wanted to limit logging. He believed forests should be protected. Many people agreed with him. Between 1911 and 1915, Wisconsin added 183,000 acres of forest reserve land.

Planting Trees

In 1911, Griffith started Wisconsin's first tree nursery. A tree nursery is a place where tree seedlings are grown. Seeds are carefully planted and watered. The trees grow until they are big enough to be moved. Then they are planted in a forest.

The first nursery in Wisconsin was at Trout Lake in Vilas County. State workers grew 192,000 conifer pine tree seedlings and 18,000 other tree seedlings there.

By 1913, many trees were ready to be planted. Workers planted 68,500 trees on state forest lands. The Trout Lake Nursery got even bigger. More seedlings were grown. A year later, half a million trees were planted.

By 1915, many acres of Cutover had been replanted. Over the next decades, they would turn back into forest land. With the help of the state forester, Wisconsin was solving the problem of the Cutover.

What is reforestation?
Reforestation means restoring land that once had trees. This involves planting seedlings after a forest has been destroyed.

A Reforestation Delay

Not everyone was happy. People in some county governments disagreed with Griffith. They didn't want Griffith to use state money to buy land in their counties. Counties collected tax money from land owners. Counties could not collect tax money for land owned by the state. People in some counties believed they would lose too much money from the forest reserve land.

In 1915, a lawsuit went to the Wisconsin Supreme Court. The court had to decide whether the state forestry department was buying land in a lawful way.

The court ruled that state money could not be used to purchase forest land. Griffith could no longer buy land for forest reserves.

Forestry in Wisconsin stopped. It looked like reforestation in Wisconsin was over. Griffith was disappointed and dismayed. He left Wisconsin in 1917.

Reforestation in the 1920s

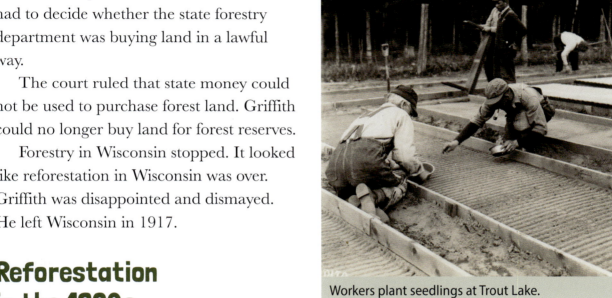
Workers plant seedlings at Trout Lake.

By the mid-1920s, many acres of Cutover had been reforested. Logging companies and paper mills began to realize that reforestation was good for business. They wanted to make sure there would be enough trees to make wood products in the future.

Companies planted tree seedlings on Cutover lands. They purchased trees from the Trout Lake Nursery. In 1928, one company planted 50,000 red and white pines. Another company planted 100,000 jack and red pine seedlings. Over time, more and more companies planted trees.

The State Helps Again

By 1924, many people realized that forests were the best solution to the Cutover problem. They knew that forests were a renewable resource that could help the Cutover lands.

The people of Wisconsin voted. The question they voted on was this: Should state money be used to buy and protect land for planting trees?

Most people voted *yes*. This allowed the state to buy and protect forest lands.

What Happened after People Voted to Protect the Forests?

- 1926: One million trees were planted.
- 1927: The Forest Crop Law was passed. The law allowed land owners to pay fewer taxes if they agreed to use their land to plant trees.
- 1927: The County Forest Reserve Law began. This helped counties start their own forests.
- 1932: The Griffith Tree Nursery opened. It was located near Wisconsin Rapids.
- 1934: The Griffith Nursery gave away more than 16.5 million trees.

Land Devoted to Forestry

Certain rules tell property owners how they can use their land. These rules are called zoning laws. Land can be zoned for different purposes, such as building a home, a business, or a farm.

Restoring the Land 111

Why Is a Forest a Renewable Resource?

A resource is something that helps humans live. A natural resource comes from nature. Water, air, and trees are some natural resources.

Trees don't just provide lumber. They also provide shade and oxygen for people and animals. They protect us from erosion and fire.

When you renew something, you make it new again or restore it to the way it used to be. Forests can be renewed because trees can be replanted. The forest can grow again. This is why a forest is a renewable resource.

In the late 1920s, counties in northern Wisconsin began passing new zoning laws. These laws changed how Cutover lands could be used. Farming on Cutover land was no longer allowed. Instead, these lands would be used for forestry.

By the end of 1937, all 24 northern counties were zoned for forestry. Now more land was available for reforestation. Conservationists (**kon** sur **vay** shuh nists) had space to put their ideas to work.

The new zoning laws meant farmers on Cutover lands needed to move. County extension agents from the University of Wisconsin helped farmers and their families find new places to live. Then the land could be turned back into forest.

A conservationist is someone who improves and protects the earth's natural resources.

Planting Trees Solves a Problem

The Great Depression was a period of hardship and hunger. It began in 1929 and lasted through the 1930s. Factories and businesses closed. Many people lost their jobs. People had very little money. Some people had little food to eat.

A forester examines Norway pines in Vilas County, Wisconsin.

During the 1930s, a huge drought dried up the southern plains of the United States, including Oklahoma and Texas. There was very little rain. The land was dry and dusty. It was almost impossible to grow food.

This part of the country had very few trees. Strong winds blew the dry topsoil into dust storms. Massive clouds of sand, dirt, and grit filled the air. The sky turned brown or red from all the dirt. During the worst dust storms, people had to stay inside.

Many dust storms happened during the Great Depression. Raging winds tore up farmland. It seemed like they would never end.

Wisconsin had dust storms, too. Dust storms raged in the central part of the state, where the soil is very sandy.

Shelterbelts helped solve the problem of the dust storms. A shelterbelt is a row of tall trees planted along the edge of a field. The trees block the wind and protect the fields. The trees also prevent sandy soils from blowing away.

The Wisconsin Conservation Department gave farmers more than 14 million trees to make shelterbelts. By 1944, almost 5,500 miles of shelterbelts were planted in Wisconsin. Planting trees helped the state solve the problem.

The Civilian Conservation Corps

During the Great Depression, many people were out of work. People could not afford food or other basic things they needed. Franklin D. Roosevelt was the president of the United States during most of the Great Depression. President Roosevelt wanted to help solve this problem.

In 1933, President Roosevelt worked with Congress to create the Civilian Conservation Corps (**kor**). It was known as the

Posters and cards encouraged tourists to visit the Northwoods. This one was made in 1932.

CCC. The CCC gave young men the chance to work and earn money. These young men lived together in camps. They took care of land owned by the government. They worked to prevent forest fires, floods, and soil erosion.

About 75,000 men worked in Wisconsin. These CCC workers worked in Chequamegon (shuh **wah** muh guhn)-Nicolet (ni koh **LAY**) National Forest, Devil's Lake State Park, Wyalusing State Park, and many other parks and forests.

CCC workers built fire lookout towers. A person in the tower watched the forest and looked for small fires. Workers put the fire out before it grew out of control.

CCC workers cleared brush to make it easier for trees to grow in the forest. They built roads and park buildings. In 1933, they planted more than 2 million trees in county forests. In 1940, they planted 25 million trees on forest land.

World War II started in 1941. The CCC closed down in 1942. Thousands of CCC workers were sent off to war.

The CCC had a lasting impact on Wisconsin. CCC workers built campgrounds and parks. They planted trees. They protected forests from fire. The CCC helped young men who had lost jobs and hope during the Great Depression.

She-She-She Camps

President Roosevelt's plan helped unemployed men all over the nation. However, the CCC was not open to women.

The president chooses people to be in charge of different parts of the government. These people are called cabinet secretaries. The president chose a woman named Frances Perkins to be in charge of the US Department of Labor. This part of the government oversees issues related to how people work. Frances Perkins was the first woman to be a cabinet secretary for a US president.

Eleanor Roosevelt was a writer and **activist** (**ak** ti vist). She and President Roosevelt were married. Eleanor Roosevelt strongly believed in equality (i **kwah** luh tee). She fought for **civil rights** and women's rights.

Eleanor Roosevelt knew that many women needed help during the Great Depression. She believed women deserved something like the CCC. Eleanor Roosevelt and Frances Perkins worked together to start a program for women. It was nicknamed the She-She-She. The first She-She-She camp opened at Bear Mountain State Park in New York.

There were about 90 She-She-She camps in the United States. Two camps were in Wisconsin. One was in Madison, and one was near Milwaukee. The camps gave women a place to learn new skills. The camps gave women hope for the future. The She-She-She camps closed in 1937.

> **activist**: someone who works toward change for something they believe in
>
> **civil rights**: a US citizen's rights of personal liberty or freedom

This picture from 1960 shows logs piled near a logging road in Brule, Wisconsin. A truck will transport the logs to a sawmill.

Chapter 14

Forestry Today

Logging still happens in Wisconsin. It has changed a lot. We have learned how to use resources from our forests without cutting down all the trees.

People still want and need products made from wood. Logging still helps Wisconsin's economy. Wood from our forests is used to make paper. Wisconsin lumber is also used for furniture, buildings, and many other things.

> In 2019, the paper industry and wood manufacturing provided more than 60,000 jobs for the people of Wisconsin.

New Inventions in Logging Equipment

The days when lumberjacks spent the winter in logging camps are far in the past. Most loggers no longer use oxen or horses. New machines have made logging safer and faster.

Chainsaws and Trucks

By the 1950s, chainsaws replaced crosscut saws. Chainsaws are handheld saws. They are powered by gasoline.

Chainsaws could cut faster than crosscut saws. Lumberjacks used chainsaws to fell trees. Then they loaded the logs onto trucks. The trucks hauled the logs to a sawmill. The chainsaw paved the way for many other inventions.

Forest Harvester and Forwarder

In the 1980s, logging crews began using the forest harvester to cut down trees and remove branches. A forest harvester is a big vehicle with a crane. A chainsaw and curved knives are attached to the end of the crane. The chainsaw cuts the tree. The knives cut off the branches.

Logging trucks changed over time. This is a logging truck from 1984.

A driver sits inside the harvester's cab. This protects them from the weather and mosquitoes. Harvesters have huge rubber tires. They can move over almost any kind of land. Harvesters can cut trees so they are all the same length. This makes it easier to transport the logs.

A vehicle called a forwarder follows the harvester. The forwarder picks up the logs. It carries the logs to a landing area where they are piled up. Then a truck transports the logs to a mill.

Harvesters and forwarders are much safer than axes, saws, and sleds. However, they are expensive. And they can leave harmful ruts in the soil.

Forwarder

Who Owns the Forest?

Today, forests cover almost half of Wisconsin.

Two-thirds of Wisconsin forest lands are privately owned by individuals, families, and companies. Many of these forests are used for logging and hunting.

One-third of Wisconsin forest land is publicly owned. This means it is owned by the government. Some is owned by the US government. Some is owned by the state, county, or town.

Public forest land is often protected from widespread logging. Animals rely on this land for habitat. People use this land for things like picnicking, walking, hiking, and camping.

Forestry at the Menominee Sawmill

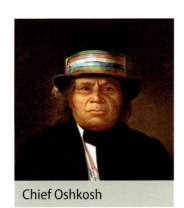
Chief Oshkosh

Menominee people have lived on the land we now call Wisconsin for 10,000 years. In the early 1800s, the Menominee people had 10 million acres of land in Wisconsin and part of Michigan. The US government took most of this land through treaties.

Today, the Menominee people have 235,000 acres of land. The Menominee **reservation** is in northeastern Wisconsin. The Wolf River runs through the reservation. Lush forests cover 93% of the land.

The water, land, and forests are sacred to the Menominee people. In 1854, Chief Oshkosh explained how they cut trees without hurting the forest:

> Start with the rising sun and work toward the setting sun, but take only the mature trees, the sick trees, and the trees that have fallen. When you reach the end of the reservation, turn and cut from the setting sun to the rising sun, and the trees will last forever.

reservation: areas of land set aside by treaty to be used by Native nations

Forestry Today 119

During the logging era, logging companies wanted to clear-cut the forests on Native reservations. The Menominee people did not want their forests to be clear-cut. They wanted to be in charge of logging on their own land.

In 1874, the US Supreme Court ruled that the Menominee and other Native nations were not allowed to cut or sell their own timber. In the 1890s, the Menominee Nation began to fight this law. The Menominee won the right to harvest trees on their own land. Other Native nations in Minnesota and Wisconsin won this right, too. But logging companies still wanted the profit for themselves.

In the end, the Menominee were successful. They worked with lawmakers in Madison to pass a law that let them continue to harvest their own timber. They also won the right to cut trees in a way that would protect the forest for the future.

The Menominee created a successful logging industry. They used the logging practices they had used in the past. They mostly cut older trees. They did not clear-cut large portions of the forest. They made sure new seedlings grew wherever trees were cut.

In 1908, the Menominee people built their own sawmill in a village called **Neopit** (nee **oh** pit). Menominee loggers cut timber and floated logs to the mill. They still use the mill today.

Their company is called Menominee Tribal Enterprises. They know where every log comes from. They cut each log by hand. They don't cut every tree.

Menominee Tribal Enterprises cuts about 15 million feet of board lumber each year. They sell wood products all over the country and world. They even supplied the boards to make

> The Menominee forest produces enough oxygen for the entire state of Wisconsin and northern Illinois!

Timber!

basketball courts for the Tokyo Olympics, March Madness, and the Milwaukee Bucks.

Menominee logging crews still follow the practices that Chief Oshkosh described. They do this with cutting-edge science. For example, they use drones to learn about the size, age, and health of the trees. This helps them decide which trees to cut.

The Menominee people have cared for their forests for thousands of years. They continue to do so today. They use resources from the forests while keeping the forests healthy. And they help people from around the world learn how to manage and preserve the forests.

What Kind of Trees Grow in Wisconsin Today?

Today, Wisconsin is home to many tree **species** (**spee** sheez). Here are some of our most common trees.

These trees are coniferous and softwood:
- balsam fir
- hemlock
- jack pine
- northern white cedar
- red pine
- white pine

These trees are deciduous and hardwood:
- American basswood
- ash
- aspen
- birch
- cherry
- maple
- oak

species: a category of living things that are similar

Sustainable Forestry

The way the Menominee people take care of the forest is called sustainable (suh **stay** nuh bul) forestry. Using something sustainably means using it in a way that does not use it up or ruin it.

Native Nations like the Menominee have always practiced sustainable forestry. Over time, other logging companies learned from the Menominee. They saw how sustainable forestry was good for the land, trees, and people.

Today, many forest owners practice sustainable forestry. They still cut down trees. However, they are careful not to cut all the trees in a forest. They do their best to keep the forest ecosystem healthy. They are careful not to harm the soil or the water.

Sustainable forestry creates a balance between the health of the environment and the needs and wants of people.

These Menominee women were part of a forestry crew. This picture was taken in 1943. World War II had started. Many Menominee men had joined the US Army. Women managed the Menominee sawmill and protected the forest.

The Apps family tree farm in Waushara County is a great example of sustainable forestry on private land. Each year, friends and family work together to plant hundreds of red pine, spruce, and jack pine by hand.

122　Timber!

The Menominee forest is big enough to be seen from outer space! This picture of northeastern Wisconsin was taken by a satellite in 2007.

National and State Forests

The US government owns a huge forest in northern Wisconsin. It is called the Chequamegon-Nicolet National Forest. The forest is a mix of hardwood and softwood trees.

The Chequamegon-Nicolet National Forest covers more than 1.5 million acres of land. It includes parts of 12 counties. This forest land was once part of the Cutover. When farmers left the Cutover, some of the land was given back to the counties. Counties sold some of that land to the US government. The government protected the land and created the national forest.

The Brule River State Forest, on a postcard from 1913

The state of Wisconsin has 10 state forests. The first state forest began with a gift from a logging company owner named Frederick Weyerhaeuser. He gave 2,840 acres of forest land to the state of Wisconsin. This created the Brule River State Forest.

Today, Wisconsin has 5.2 million acres of publicly owned forests. These forests are owned and managed by the US government, the state, counties, and towns.

School Forests

In 1925, Harry Russell was in charge of the College of Agriculture at the University of Wisconsin. Russell found a creative way to help bring the forest back to northern Wisconsin. He

> 4-H is an organization for kids and teens. 4-H members do projects in science, health, and agriculture. The four Hs stand for Head, Heart, Hands, and Health.

suggested that children plant trees in the Cutover lands as a school project.

At the same time, a man named Wakelin McNeel was helping children in the 4-H program learn about nature.

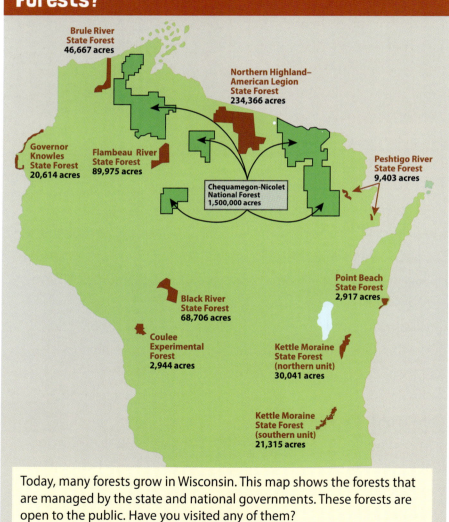

Today, many forests grow in Wisconsin. This map shows the forests that are managed by the state and national governments. These forests are open to the public. Have you visited any of them?

McNeel began working with kids and their teachers to plant trees. Because the trees were planted by schoolchildren, the land was called a school forest. McNeel knew that when children spend time outside, they learn to appreciate nature. He wanted children to have the experience of planting trees. This would help them learn the habit of caring for the environment.

Russell and McNeel believed school forests could help repair the Cutover *and* help young people become conservationists.

Wakelin McNeel was known as Ranger Mac. He worked with students all over Wisconsin. This picture shows Ranger Mac visiting a school in 1952. For 21 years, he also hosted a popular radio show to help kids learn about conservation. It was called "Afield with Ranger Mac."

Russell went to state lawmakers with an idea. He wanted school districts to be able to own land and use it for forestry programs. Lawmakers agreed. In 1927, they passed Russell's idea into law.

McNeel helped school districts start their own forests. The first three school forests were created in the spring of 1928. They were in Laona, Crandon, and Wabeno, Wisconsin. All three were in the Cutover region.

In 1935, Wisconsin lawmakers passed a law about teaching conservation. It stated that conservation must be taught in all public elementary, middle, and high schools. Wisconsin was the first state in the country to require students to learn about conservation.

Today, there are more than 300 school forests in Wisconsin. They are located in every county in the state.

Chapter 15

The Future of the Forests

Why should we remember the logging era in Wisconsin? Our state's pine forests played a key role in building our country. Many settlers used Wisconsin lumber. By the late 1800s, Wisconsin lumber was used all over the nation. It became homes, barns, sidewalks, furniture, boats, and paper products.

Learning about the history of logging can help us take better care of the land and trees in the future.

Why Do People Value Trees?

What would Wisconsin be without its forests? To value something is to decide it is important. What we value can change over time.

Today, people value Wisconsin's forests for many reasons. Our state has millions of acres of forest land. Millions more trees grow in towns and cities. No matter where you live, Wisconsin trees are important.

Trees Make Us Healthy

Trees are good for our health. Trees remove pollution from the air. This makes the air healthier for us to breathe. Trees give us shade from the sun. This keeps our skin healthy. Trees make the air cooler. This makes it safer for us to spend time outside.

Spending time outdoors improves our emotional and physical health. The simple act of being in nature makes people feel happier and less stressed.

Trees Help the Environment

Forest trees provide a habitat for wildlife. Urban trees provide homes for wildlife, too. They are a place for birds and squirrels to nest.

Tree roots protect the land from erosion. Trees help reduce water runoff that can cause rivers and sewers to overflow. And trees help keep the air and water healthy.

Trees Are Good for the Economy

Wisconsin trees are used to make many wood products that we buy today. These include lumber, grocery bags, cardboard boxes, and paper.

In 1910, high school students from Wisconsin competed in a poster contest to promote conservation. A student from Superior painted this poster.

Many animal species rely on the forest and rivers for food and shelter in every season of the year.

Trees also help lower the amount of money people need to spend on electricity. Large trees can provide enough shade to keep a home cool inside. This helps people use less air-conditioning in the summer.

Trees Are Beautiful

Trees provide **aesthetic** (es **the** tik) value. This means we appreciate their beauty.

aesthetic: beautiful or nice to look at

The Future of the Forests

When you visit a forest, you can appreciate its beauty in all seasons. You can admire the changing colors of leaves in the fall. You can feel the crunch of snow on a forest trail in the winter. You can marvel at the bloom on the forest floor in the spring. And you can enjoy the cool shade of the **tree canopy** in the summer.

Juniper Rock Overlook

Springtime wildflowers

tree canopy: the uppermost spreading layer of a forest

Trees help make towns and cities beautiful, too. Trees improve the way city streets and neighborhoods look and feel.

Trees Help Us Have Fun

Parks give us places to play, walk, picnic, and get together with family and friends. Forests give us places to hike, camp, hunt, and ski. Forest lakes give us places to boat and swim.

A lot of people have fun in nature. However, sometimes they can harm the environment. Campers can leave trash behind. Motorboats can leak gasoline into lakes. Hikers can trample through fragile ecosystems.

Ecotourism (**ee** koh **tur** i zuhm) is a kind of tourism that reduces this harmful impact. Ecotourism helps people enjoy

Trees provide shade in city parks and playgrounds.

The Future of the Forests

nature in ways that protect the environment. Examples of ecotourism are visiting a nature preserve or riding a bike on a trail through the woods.

Trees Are Educational

Trees help us learn. Playing, working, and spending time outside helps us understand the natural world. Places such as parks, nature centers, and school forests help kids explore the plants, animals, and habitats of wooded areas.

Trees Have a Cultural Connection

Trees are an important part of many people's cultural beliefs and traditions. Some beliefs and traditions are related to harvesting fruits, nuts, or sap from trees. Others are related to the spiritual meaning of trees and forests.

A particular tree, park, or forest may have special memories or meanings for people. Returning to this place helps people find peace and a sense of well-being.

What Is a Forest Steward?

Many people worked together to solve the problems after too many trees were cut down. The forests will stay healthy as long as enough people care about them. You can be one of those people.

A forest steward (**stoo** urd) is someone who cares about the future health of our forests. Forest stewards think about what we can do today that will help our environment for many years to come. Forest stewards care about all the living and nonliving parts of a forest. They protect the forest for future generations.

How will you help? You can be a forest steward! Want to find out how? See the checklist on page 135 for a list of ideas.

Student volunteers trim trees in the Chippewa National Forest. They are part of a group called Urban Roots, in St. Paul, Minnesota. Urban Roots helps young people learn about environmental careers.

A forest steward learns about forests. A forest steward uses critical thinking, learns from many sources, and studies the past to make decisions about the future. A forest steward works to change things that can harm a forest ecosystem.

Anyone can be a forest steward. You don't need to wait until you're an adult. You don't need to go to a special school. If you care about the forest, you can learn to be a forest steward today.

When people take action to help the environment, that is called stewardship (**stoo** urd ship). Acts of stewardship can be as simple, like picking up trash in a park.

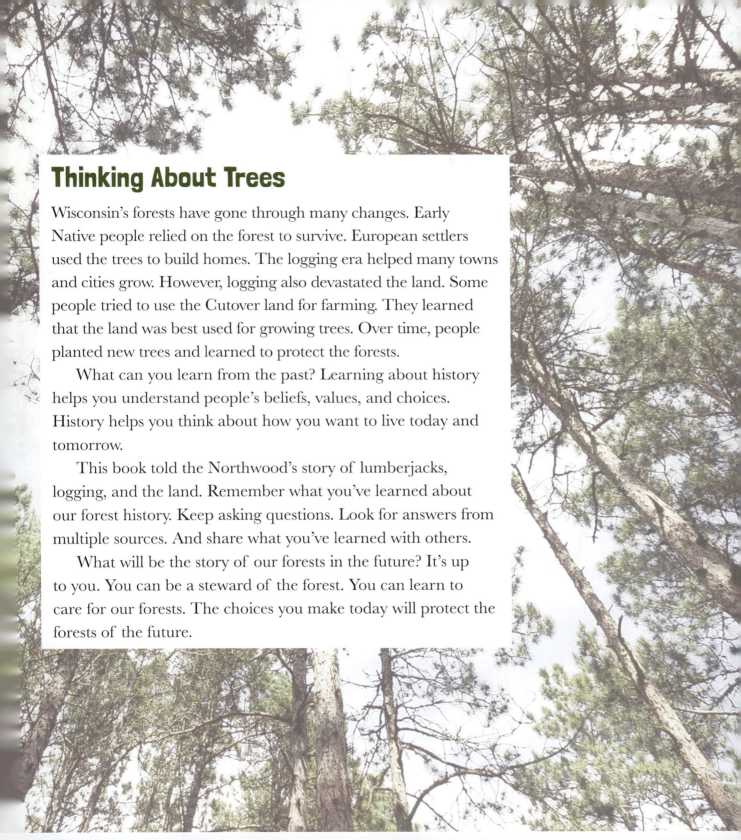

Thinking About Trees

Wisconsin's forests have gone through many changes. Early Native people relied on the forest to survive. European settlers used the trees to build homes. The logging era helped many towns and cities grow. However, logging also devastated the land. Some people tried to use the Cutover land for farming. They learned that the land was best used for growing trees. Over time, people planted new trees and learned to protect the forests.

What can you learn from the past? Learning about history helps you understand people's beliefs, values, and choices. History helps you think about how you want to live today and tomorrow.

This book told the Northwood's story of lumberjacks, logging, and the land. Remember what you've learned about our forest history. Keep asking questions. Look for answers from multiple sources. And share what you've learned with others.

What will be the story of our forests in the future? It's up to you. You can be a steward of the forest. You can learn to care for our forests. The choices you make today will protect the forests of the future.

CHECKLIST

How to Be a Steward for the Trees

There are so many ways YOU can help trees and forests! Pick an idea from this list to get started:

- ☐ Visit a forest or a park. Take a walk through the trees. Listen to the wind moving through the branches.
- ☐ Learn the names of trees. You can identify trees by their leaves and bark.
- ☐ Choose a tree and observe it for a year. When do the leaves fall off? When do buds form in the spring? What changes do you see? What else do you notice? Write down your observations in a notebook.
- ☐ Pay attention to the weather. On a hot day, compare the temperature in the shade of a tree with the temperature in the sunshine. See how the weather affects the trees.
- ☐ Observe wildlife. Many small animals live near trees. In the winter, you can learn to identify animal tracks in the snow.
- ☐ Be a bird watcher. Watch how trees help protect bird nests.
- ☐ Investigate a fallen tree. What insects live there? How long does it take for the tree to begin to decay?
- ☐ Plant wildflower seeds.
- ☐ Gather small branches, leaves, acorns, sticks, pine needles, pinecones, and other nature items. Make a collage or build something with them. What can you create?
- ☐ Investigate the ways bees and other pollinators help trees.
- ☐ Raise money to plant a tree in your schoolyard.
- ☐ Build and hang birdhouses. Provide water for the birds.

- ☐ Pick up litter in your neighborhood.
- ☐ Look for trees with broken branches. Sometimes this can happen after a storm. Show a grownup so they can trim the broken branches and make sure the tree is healthy.
- ☐ Reduce, reuse, and recycle. Find ways to reuse paper.
- ☐ Spend time "stump sitting." Find a quiet place in a park or forest. Listen, think, write in a journal, or draw what you see.
- ☐ Remind your friends not to break branches off of trees.
- ☐ In the spring, smell tree blossoms. Watch for pollinators near the blossoms.
- ☐ Celebrate Earth Day with your family or school. (Earth Day started in Wisconsin!)
- ☐ Learn about a conservation group. Many groups in Wisconsin and around the world are working to protect our environment. Learn how you can help their work.
- ☐ Teach someone else how they can be a steward for the trees, too.
- ☐ Start a Stewardship Club in your school or neighborhood.
- ☐ _____

(add your own ideas to the list!)

Learn More

A steam logging engine on display at the Mid-Continent Railway Museum in North Freedom, Wisconsin

A boardwalk in the Chequamegon-Nicolet National Forest

Books for Young Readers

Allison, R. Bruce. *If Trees Could Talk: Stories about Wisconsin Trees.* Madison: Wisconsin Historical Society Press, 2009.

Apps-Bodilly, Susan. *Seeds in Soil: Planting a Garden and Finding Your Roots.* Madison: Wisconsin Historical Society Press, 2022.

Loew, Patty. *Native People of Wisconsin,* Revised and Expanded. Madison: Wisconsin Historical Society Press, 2015.

Malone, Bobbie. *Learning from the Land: Wisconsin Land Use*, 2nd Edition. Madison: Wisconsin Historical Society Press, 2011.

Zimm, John. *John Nelligan, Wisconsin Lumberjack*. Madison: Wisconsin Historical Society Press, 2015.

Websites

EEK! Environmental Education for Kids (in Spanish and English)
https://www.eekwi.org/activities

Forest Frenzy: The Giving Forest, educational game for students
https://kylelev.itch.io/forset-frenzy

National Junior Ranger Booklets
https://www.nps.gov/kids/junior-rangers.htm

Turning Points in Wisconsin History
http://www.wisconsinhistory.org/turningpoints

Educational Resources

Forestry Educational Resources from the Wisconsin Department of Natural Resources
https://dnr.wisconsin.gov/education/forests

Library of Congress Getting Started with Primary Sources
https://www.loc.gov/programs/teachers/getting-started-with-primary-sources/

Stanford History Education Group—Reading Like a Historian History Lessons
https://sheg.stanford.edu/history-lessons

Wisconsin Center for Environmental Education, University of Wisconsin–Stevens Point
https://www.uwsp.edu/wcee/wcee/

Wisconsin Department of Public Instruction Environmental Education Resources
https://dpi.wi.gov/environmental-ed

Wisconsin First Nations Education Materials
https://wisconsinfirstnations.org/

Wisconsin School Forests
https://www.uwsp.edu/wcee/wcee/leaf/sf/

Outdoor Places to Explore

Aldo Leopold Nature Center
    Monona, WI
    https://aldoleopoldnaturecenter.org/

Bay Beach Wildlife Sanctuary
    Green Bay, WI
    https://www.greenbaywi.gov/1418/Bay-Beach-Wildlife-Sanctuary

Chequamegon-Nicolet National Forest
    https://www.fs.usda.gov/cnnf

The Ridges Sanctuary
    Bailey's Harbor, WI
    https://www.ridgessanctuary.org/

Riveredge Nature Center
    Saukville, WI
    https://www.riveredgenaturecenter.org/

Schlitz Audubon Nature Center
    Bayside, WI
    https://www.schlitzaudubon.org/

Wisconsin's Ice Age Trail
    https://www.iceagetrail.org/

Wisconsin State Parks
    https://dnr.wisconsin.gov/topic/Parks

Other Places to Visit

Chippewa Valley Museum and Wisconsin Logging Museum
    Eau Claire, WI
    https://www.cvmuseum.com/

Forest History Center
    Grand Rapids, MN
    https://www.mnhs.org/foresthistory

Hartwick Pines Logging Museum at Hartwick Pines State Park
  Grayling, MI
  https://www.michigan.gov/mhc/museums/hp

Higgins Lake Nursery and CCC Museum
  Roscommon, MI
  https://www.michigan.gov/mhc/museums/hln-ccc

Lumberjack Steam Train and Camp 5 Museum
  Laona, WI
  https://www.lumberjacksteamtrain.com/

MacKenzie Center, Logging Museum and Sawmill Exhibit
  Poynette, WI
  https://dnr.wisconsin.gov/education/mackenzie/museums

Madeline Island Museum
  La Pointe, WI
  https://madelineislandmuseum.wisconsinhistory.org/

Menominee Indian Tribe and Logging Camp Museum
  Keshena, WI
  https://www.menominee-nsn.gov/CulturePages/CulturalMuseum.aspx

Mid-Continent Railway Museum
  North Freedom, WI
  https://www.midcontinent.org/

Museum of Ojibwa Culture
  St. Ignace, MI
  https://museumofojibwaculture.net/

National Railroad Museum
  Green Bay, WI
  https://nationalrrmuseum.org/

Neville Public Museum
  Green Bay, WI
  https://www.nevillepublicmuseum.org/

Old World Wisconsin
   Eagle, WI
   https://oldworldwisconsin.wisconsinhistory.org/

Onalaska Area Historical Museum, Logging Exhibit (Located in the Onalaska Public Library)
   Onalaska, WI
   https://lacrossecounty.org/library/libraries/onalaska

Ozaukee County Pioneer Village
   Saukville, WI
   https://www.ochs.co.ozaukee.wi.us/pioneer-village

Peshtigo Fire Museum
   Peshtigo, WI
   http://www.peshtigofiremuseum.com/

Pioneer Park Historical Complex and Logging Museum
   Rhinelander, WI
   https://rhinelanderpphc.com/

Stonefield Village and Agriculture Museum
   Cassville, WI
   https://stonefield.wisconsinhistory.org/

Urban Ecology Center
   Milwaukee, WI
   https://urbanecologycenter.org/

Wisconsin History Center
   Madison, WI
   https://historicalmuseum.wisconsinhistory.org/

Pronunciation Guide

a: cat (kat), plaid (plad), half (haf), laugh (laf)

ah: father (**fah** THur), heart (hahrt), dark (dahrk), sergeant (**sahr** juhnt)

air: dairy (**dair** ee), care (kair), carry (**kair** ee), berry (**bair** ee), bury (**bair** ee), bear (bair), air (air), prayer (prair), where (whair), their (THair)

aw: all (awl), walk (wawk), taught (tawt), law (law), broad (brawd), bought (bawt)

ay: say (say), page (payj), break (brayk), aid (ayd), neighbor (**nay** bur), they (THay), vein (vayn), gauge (gayj)

e: bet (bet), says (sez), deaf (def), friend (frend), many (**men** ee), said (sed), leopard (**lep** urd)

ee: bee (bee), team (teem), fear (feer), even, (**ee** vuhn), receive (ri **ceev**), people (**pee** puhl), relieve (ri **leev**), key (kee), machine (muh **sheen**), phoenix (**fee** niks)

i: bit (bit), busy, (**biz** ee), been (bin), sieve (siv), women (**wim** uhn), build (bild), hymn (him), England (**ing** gluhnd)

I: Ice (Is), lie (lI), bye (bI), aye (I), height (hIt), high (hI), eye (I), buy (bI), sky (skI)

o: odd (od), hot (hot), watch (wotch), honest (**hon** ist)

oh: bureau (**byur** hoh), open (**oh** puhn), oh (oh), sew (soh), boat (boht), toe (toh), low (loh), brooch (brohch), soul (sohl), though (THoh)

oi: boil (boil), boy (boi)

oo: pool (pool), move (moov), shoe (shoo), through (throo), rule (rool), blue (bloo), fruit (froot), threw (throo), maneuver (muh **noo** vur)

or: order (**or** dur), more (mor)

ou: house (hous), bough (bou), now (nou)

u: good (gud), should (shud), full, (ful)

Pronunciation Guide 143

uh: cup (kuhp), come (cuhm), does (duhz), flood (fluhd), trouble (**truhb** uhl), motion (**mo** shun), comma (**kom** uh), magician (mah **jish** uhn), women (**wim** uhn), button (**buht** uhn)

ur: burn (burn), pearl (purl), stern (sturn), bird (burd), worker (**wurk** ur), journey (**jur** nee), myrtle (**mur** tuhl), measure (**mezh** ur)

yoo: use (yooz), cue (kyoo), you (yoo), few (fyoo), beauty (**byoo** tee), view (vyoo), feud (fyood)

b: bad (bad), rabbit (**rab** it)

ch: child (chIld), watch, (wahch), future (**fyoo** chur), question (**kwes** chuhn), righteous (**rI** chuhs)

d: dog (dawg), add (ad), billed (bild)

f: fad (fad), effort (**ef** urt), laugh (laf), phone (fohn)

g: get (get), egg (eg), ghost (gohst), guest (gest), catalogue (**kat** uh lawg)

h: hot (hot), who (hoo)

j: joy (joi), badger (**baj** ur), soldier (**sol** jur), magic (**maj** ik), exaggerate (eg **zaj** uh rayt)

k: kind, (kInd), coat (koht), back (bak), folk (fohk), account (uh **kount**), acquire (uh **kwIr**), chemist (**kem** ist)

l: like (lIk), tell (tel)

m: me (mee), common (**com** uhn), calm (kahm), climb (klIm), solemn (**sol** uhm)

n: net (net), dinner (**din** ur), knife (nIf), pneumonia (noo **moh** nyuh), gnaw (naw)

ng: long (lawng), ink (ingk), tongue (tuhng)

p: cap (kap), happy (**hap** ee)

r: run (ruhn), carry (**kair** ee), wrong (rawng), rhyme (rIm)

s: say (say), cent (sent), scent (sent), miss (mis), twice (twIs), psychology (sI **kahl** uh jee)

t: tell (tel), bottom (**bot** uhm), stepped (stept), caught (kawt), Thomas (**tom** uhs), pterodactyl (ter uh **dak** tuhl)

th: thank (thangk)

TH: that (THat), breathe (breeTH)

v: vain (vayn), of (uhv)

w: web (web), quick (kwik), choir (kwIr), what (wuht)

y: yet (yet), opinion (oh **pin** yuhn), hallelujah (hal uh **loo** yuh)

z: zero (**zir** oh), has (haz), buzz (buhz), busy (**biz** ee), scissor (**siz** ur), xylophone (**zI** luh fohn)

zh: measure (**mezh** ur), azure (**azh** ur), garage (guh **razh**), division (duh **vizh** uhn)

Glossary

acre (**ay** kur): a measurement of land about the size of a football field

activist (**ak** ti vist): someone who works towards change for something they believe in

adapted (uh **dap** tid): changed or adjusted to fit different conditions

aesthetic (es **the** tik): beautiful or nice to look at

anvil: a heavy block made of iron

artifact (**ar** ti fakt): an object from a particular time period

bateau (ba **toh**): a flat-bottomed boat

bedrolls: bedding that is rolled up for carrying

blacksmith: a person who makes or repairs things made of iron or steel

board foot: a piece of lumber that is one foot wide, one foot long, and one inch thick

coal (**kohl**): a solid black mineral that is mined and used for fuel

cede (**seed**): give up

civil rights: a US citizen's rights of personal liberty or freedom

clear-cutting: the removal of all trees in an area of forest

climate (**clI** muht): the average condition of the weather over time

coniferous (koh **ni** fur es): a kind of tree that has cones and needles

conservationist (**kon** sur **vay** shuh nist): a person who helps protect natural resources

Cutover (**kuht** oh vur): the name given to land that had all of its trees cut down by logging companies

current: part of a body of water that moves in a certain direction

Glossary

dam: a barrier that holds back the flow of water

deciduous (di **si** juh wuhs): a kind of tree that has leaves that fall off in autumn

drought (**drout**): a period of time with very little rain

economy (i **kah** nuh mee): the goods, services, and money that are made and used by a group of people

ecosystem (**ee** koh si stuhm): a community of living things and their environment

ecotourism (**ee** koh **tur** i zuhm): tourism designed to reduce harm to the environment

erosion (i **roh** zhen): the act of wearing away, often by wind or water

exaggerated (ig **za** juh ray tuhd): described as larger or greater than what is true

fell: cut down

flammable: easy to catch on fire

foraged (**for** ijd): searched for food

forest reserve: area of forest protected by the government in which trees cannot be cut down for profit

forester: a person who practices forestry and manages forest lands

forestry: the science of growing and taking care of trees in forests

forge (**forj**): a fireplace used for heating metals

glaciers (**glay** shurz): giant sheets of ice formed in mountain valleys or near the North and South Poles

goods: things that are made to be sold or traded

growing season: the length of time crops need to grow

immigrants: people from one country who move to settle in another

industry: a type of business

inferno (in **fur** noh): a fire that cannot be stopped

legislature (**lej** uh slay chur): a group of people who make laws

locomotive (**loh** kuh **moh** tiv): an engine that moves by its own power

manipulated (muh **ni** pyuh **lay** ted): changed in a way that is untrue

mechanical (mi **ka** ni kuhl): made or operated by a machine

origin story: what a culture believes about how the world began

peak (**peek**): the highest or busiest point

permanently: not brief or temporary

persuade (pur **swayd**): to win over to a belief or way of acting

processed (**prah** sest): prepared or changed by a series of steps

pulleys (**pul** eez): a tool used to lift or lower heavy objects

reforestation (ree **for** uh **stay** shuhn): renewing a forest by planting young trees or seeds

renewable resource: a natural resource that replaces the portion taken by humans or environmental disasters

reservation: areas of land set aside to be used by Native nations

revolution (re vuh **loo** shuhn): a big shift or change

sawmill: a place where logs are sawed into boards and sold

shelterbelts: rows of tall trees planted along the edge of a field

skid: to haul something by dragging it

sluiced (**sloost**): directed logs through water

species (**spee** sheez): a category of living things that are similar

steward (**stoo** urd): someone who cares for something

surveyed (**sur** vayd): examined the condition or value

sustainable (suh **stay** nuh bul): using a resource in such a way that it is not used up or ruined

territory: a piece of land that belongs to the US but is not a state

topsoil: the top layer of soil

treaties (tree **teez**): agreements between nations describing certain rights and rules

tree canopy: the uppermost spreading layer of a forest

tree nursery: a place where trees are grown from seed so they can be planted in a forest

Acknowledgments

Many people helped with this book. Thank you to Steve Apps, photographer, for his photographs and his editing of family images. Thank you to Kerry Bloedorn of the Pioneer Park Historical Complex Logging Museum, Rhinelander. Thank you to the Onalaska Area Historical Museum. Thank you to the staff at the Wisconsin Historical Society Press, including Kate Thompson, Kristin Gilpatrick, Carrie Kilman, Kaitlyn Hein, Maria Parrott-Ryan, and John Ferguson.

Bibliography

Apps, Jerry. *The Civilian Conservation Corps in Wisconsin*. Madison: Wisconsin Historical Society Press, 2019.

Apps, Jerry. *Mills of Wisconsin and the Midwest*. Madison: Tamarack Press, 1980.

Apps, Jerry. *When the White Pine Was King, A History of Lumberjacks, Log Drives, and Sawdust Cities in Wisconsin*. Madison: Wisconsin Historical Society Press, 2020.

Apps, Jerry. *Wisconsin Agriculture: A History*. Madison: Wisconsin Historical Society Press, 2015.

Pferdehirt, Julia. *Wisconsin Forest Tales*. Black Earth, WI: Trails Custom Printing, 2004.

Rodriguez, Noreen Naseem. *Social Studies for a Better World, An Anti-Oppressive Approach for Elementary Educators*. New York: W. W. Norton & Company, 2022.

Rosholt, Malcolm. *The Wisconsin Logging Book, 1839–1939*. Rosholt, WI: Rosholt House, 1980.

Rucker, Della. *A History of Logging in Oconto County*. Oconto, WI: Oconto County Economic Development Corporation, 1999.

Sorden, L. G., and Jacque Vallier. *Lumberjack Lingo*. Minocqua, WI: North Word, 1986.

Trosper, Ronald L. "Indigenous Influence on Forest Management on the Menominee Indian Reservation." *Forest and Ecology Management* 249, nos. 1–2 (2007): 134–139. https://doi.org/10.1016/j.foreco.2007.04.037.

Yazzie, Victoria. "The Tribal Perspective of Old Growth in Frequent-Fire Forests—Its History." *Ecology and Society* 12, no. 2 (2007). http://www.jstor.org/stable/26267893.

Illustration Credits

Front Matter **PAGE ii** Two lumberjacks, WHI Image ID 106379. **PAGE vi** Header image, photo by Victor Kilman.

Introduction **Page viii** Header image, photo by Steve Apps; The author as a child, family photo courtesy of Susan Apps-Bodilly. **PAGE x** Trail through the woods, WHI Image ID 129196.

Chapter 1 **PAGE 3** Building a canoe, WHI Image ID 114336. **PAGE 5** Neighbors sawing wood, WHI Image ID 73841. **PAGE 7** Forest view, photo by Carrie Kilman.

Chapter 2 **PAGE 10** Sawing a tree, WHI Image ID 58531. **PAGE 11** Lambeau Field, photo by Ryan Dickey, Creative Commons. **PAGE 12** Deciduous trees in autumn, photo by Karen Hine; Coniferous trees in winter, photo by Steve Apps.

Chapter 3 **PAGE 14** White pine forest, photo by Nicholas A. Tonelli, Creative Commons. **PAGE 15** Outside of a logging camp, WHI Image ID 94178. **PAGE 16** Inside a bunkhouse, WHI Image ID 83371. **PAGE 17** Buildings in a logging camp, WHI Image ID 64784. **PAGE 18** Lumberjacks eating, WHI Image ID 5777. **PAGE 19** Pile of logs, photo by Steve Apps.

Chapter 4 **PAGE 21** Group of lumberjacks, WHI Image ID 94170. **PAGE 22** Blacksmith, Farm Security Administration Photograph Collection, Library of Congress, Prints and Photographs Division. **PAGE 24** Two lumberjacks felling a tree, photo by John Fletcher Ford, courtesy of Oregon State University Library Special Collections and Archives. **PAGE 25** Crew with oxen and horses, WHI Image ID 4176. **PAGE 28** Logging crew, WHI Image ID 5825.

Chapter 5 **PAGE 30** Logging crew in Sawyer County, WHI Image ID 91604; Red and black plaid, photo by Mike McDonald, courtesy of Ember Studio. **PAGE 31** Cook and cookee, WHI Image ID 1962. **PAGE 33** Metal dishes, photo by Susan Apps-Bodilly; Dinner at a logging camp, WHI Image ID 3438. **PAGE 34** Women and children, WHI Image ID 94222.

Chapter 6 **PAGE 39** Using a crosscut saw, WHI Image ID 2413. **PAGE 40** Skidding tongs, photo by Susan Apps-Bodilly. **PAGE 41** Logging scene, WHI Image ID 2775. **PAGE 42** Loading a sled, WHI Image ID 148643. **PAGE 44** List of logging marks, photo by Susan Apps-Bodilly. **PAGE 45** Marked logs, photo by Susan Apps-Bodilly.

Chapter 7 **PAGE 46** Reading a book, WHI Image ID 127215. **PAGE 47** Fiddler and dancer, WHI Image ID 55608. **PAGE 48** Hodag sculpture, WHI Image ID 149422. **PAGE 50** Paul Bunyan drawing, WHI Image ID 55609. **PAGE 51** Statue of Paul Bunyan and Babe, Carol M. Highsmith Archive, Library of Congress, Prints and Photographs Division; Washing clothes, WHI Image ID 24425.

Chapter 8 **PAGE 54** Log drivers on a big log, WHI Image ID 37826. **PAGE 55** Log driver with peavey, WHI Image ID 46149. **PAGE 56** Log drive mural, photo by Susan Apps-Bodilly. **PAGE 57** Bateau boats, WHI Image ID 2208. **PAGE 59** "Dancing Annie" wanigan, WHI Image ID 119881.

Chapter 9 **PAGE 60** Log drivers eating lunch, WHI Image ID 77924. **PAGE 63** Man in a logjam, WHI Image ID 115693. **PAGE 65** Logjam postcard, WHI Image ID 112342.

149

PAGE 66 Auger, photo by Steve Apps. **PAGE 67** HH Bennett photo of raft tied with rope, WHI Image ID 6680.

Chapter 10 **PAGE 70** Sawmill workers lining up logs, WHI Image ID 12325. **PAGE 73** Waterwheel, Pixabay. **PAGE 76** Up and down saw, illustration by Eric Sloane, originally published in *A Reverence for Wood*. **PAGE 77** Using a circular saw, WHI Image ID 83241. **PAGE 78** Band saw, Canadian Forest Industries. **PAGE 79** Two boys log rolling, photo by Steve Apps.

Chapter 11 **PAGE 81** Steamboat postcard, WHI Image ID 132078. **PAGE 82** Steam-powered trains, WHI Image ID 5771. **PAGE 84** Steam log hauler, WHI Image ID 5820. **PAGE 85** Train depot, WHI Image ID 24986.

Chapter 12 **PAGE 88** Cutover, WHI Image ID 105729. **PAGE 89** Lumberjacks on logs, WHI Image ID 1939; Increase Lapham, WHI Image ID 99872. **PAGE 92** Soil erosion, WHI Image ID 3991. **PAGE 93** Family in field, WHI Image ID 1881. **PAGE 94** Map of Peshtigo Fire, WHI Image ID 101577. **PAGE 98** Filbert Roth's map, WHI Image ID 119926.

Chapter 13 **PAGE 103** Tall tale postcard, WHI Image ID 95148. **PAGE 104** Pulling stumps, WHI Image ID 1915. **PAGE 105** Blowing up a stump, WHI Image ID 78988. **PAGE 109** Planting seedlings, WHI Image ID 42525. **PAGE 112** Forester with pines, WHI Image ID 131502. **PAGE 113** CCC postcard, WHS Image ID 5762. **PAGE 115** Logs piled near road, WHS Image ID 108332.

Chapter 14 **PAGE 117** Logging truck, WHI Image ID 84213; Forwarder, photo by Steve Apps. **PAGE 118** Chief Oshkosh, WHI Image ID 1888. **PAGE 121** Menominee women's crew, WHI Image ID 35126; Planting at Apps family farm, photo by Steve Apps. **PAGE 122** Forest from space, NASA image by Jeff Schmaltz. **PAGE 123** Brule River State Forest postcard, WHI Image ID 82907. **PAGE 125** Ranger Mac with students, University of Wisconsin–Madison Archives, Madison, Wisconsin.

Chapter 15 **PAGE 127** Conserve poster, WHI Image ID 118363. **PAGE 128** Black bear, photo by Rebecca Huncilman, USDA Forest Service; Whooping crane family, photo by Jill Utrup, US Fish and Wildlife Service Midwest Region; Fawn, photo by Steve Apps. **PAGE 129** Juniper Rock Overlook, photo by Katie Lemoine, USDA Forest Service; Spring flowers, photo by Max Leveridge, USDA Forest Service. **PAGE 130** City park, photo by Ray Bouknight, Creative Commons. **PAGE 131** Students trimming trees, USDA Forest Service, Eastern Region. **PAGE 134** Tall trees, WHI Image ID 68498.

Back Matter **PAGE 137** Header image, photo by Victor Kilman; Steam logging engine, Carol M. Highsmith Archive, Library of Congress, Prints and Photographs Division; Forest boardwalk photo by Rebecca Geyer, USDA Forest Service.

Index

When you see a page number in **bold**, it means there is a picture or a map on the page.

A
activists, 115
aesthetic value of trees, 128–130, **129**
Alft, William, 32
animals
    farm animals, 102, 106
    in logging camps, 22, **22**, 25, **25**, **41**, **42**
    wildlife, 2, 4, 95, 118, 127, **128**
anvils, 18
artifacts, 26
augers, 66, **66**
axes, 24, 37

B
band saws, 78, **78**
barn bosses, 22
barns, 17
bateau boats, 57, **57**
Bear Mountain State Park, 115
beauty of trees, 128–130, **129**
beaver pelts, 4
bedrolls, 58
blacksmiths, 18, 22–23, **22**
blacksmith shops, 18
bobsleds, 41–42, **42**
bookkeepers/clerks, 23
Brule River State Forest, 123, **123**
buckers, 24
bunkhouses, 16–17, **16**

C
canoes, 2, **3**
cant hooks, 42
chainsaws, 116–117
Chequamegon-Nicolet National Forest, 114, 122, **137**
Chippewa Falls, Wisconsin, 86
choppers, 24
circular saws, 76, **77**
Civilian Conservation Corps (CCC), **113**, 113–114
civil rights, 115
clear-cutting, 84
clerks/bookkeepers, 23
climate
    and farming, 106
    prehistoric, 2
clothing for logging crews, 29–30, 54
coal, 18
coniferous trees, 12, **12**, 120

151

conservation, 111, **127**
cookees, 23, 30–31, **31**
cookhouses, 18, **18**
cooks, 23, 30–31, **31**
County Forest Reserve Law, 110
crosscut saws, 38, **39**, **41**
cutover land
    Chequamegon-Nicolet National Forest, 122
    and farming, 102–106
    history of, **88**, 89–101, **90**, **92**
    map of, **100**
    problem of, 106–107
    school forests, 125
    stump removal, **104**, 104–105

D

Dakota Nation, 7
darning socks, 46
debarking process, 72–73
deciduous trees, 12, **12**, 120
Devil's Lake State Park, 114
draft horses, 25, **25**
dust storms, 112
dynamite, 64, 105, **105**

E

Eau Claire, Wisconsin, 86
economy
    local, 101
    value of trees, 127–128

ecosystems, 95
ecotourism, 130–131
erosion, **92**, 96
Europeans
    settlers, 4–5, 10, 20, 104, 133
    trading with Native peoples, 4

F

farmers and farming, 4, 102–106, **103**, 111
felling trees, **10**, 24, **24**, 37–39, **39**
fires
    dangers of, 76, **92**, 96–97
    fire lookout towers, 114
    Peshtigo Fire, 93–95, **93**, **94**
fitters, 24
floating kitchens, 58, **59**
Fond du Lac, Wisconsin, 86
food in logging camps, 29–33
foraging, 2
foremen
    logging camps, 23–24
    sawmills, 71
Forest Crop Law, 110
forest harvesters, 117
forest reserves, 107

forestry, 107–108
    future of, 126–133
    land devoted to, 110–111
    reforestation, 107–109, **109**
    sustainable forestry, 121–122
    today, 116–125
forestry law, 107
forest stewards, 131–132, **132**, 135–136
forges, 18
forwarders, 117, **117**
4-H programs, 123–124

G

gang saws, 76–77
glaciers, 1
go-devil, 40
Great Depression, 111–113
Great Plains, 10
Griffith, Edward Merriam, 107–109
Griffith Tree Nursery, 110

H

hardwood, 12, 120
hardwood forests, 83–84
Ho-Chunk Nation, 2, 7
Hodag, 48–49, **48**
Horses, 25, **25**

I

immigrants, 4, 20

K

Koehler, Julius, 103

L

La Crosse, Wisconsin, 86
land ownership/land use, 118
    Native Nations' rights to harvest trees, 119
    public vs. private land, 118
    zoning laws, 110–111
Lapham, Increase, **90**, 90–91, 97
Lincoln, Ceylon Childs, 68–69
locomotives, 82–83
log drives, 52–59
    bateau boats, 57, **57**
    floating kitchens, 58, **59**
    front crews, 54–56, **54, 56**
    night booms, 58
    rear crews, 56–57
    river highways, 52–54, 55
logging
    clear-cutting, 84, **88, 90**
    fire, dangers of, **92**, 93–95, 96–97
    hardwood forests, 83–84
    impact on ecosystems, 95–99
logging camps, 13–19, **15, 17, 51**
    barns, 17
    blacksmith shops, 18
    bunkhouses, 16–17, **16**
    cookhouses, 18, **18**
    outhouses, 17
    stores, 18
    women, 34–36, **34**
logging companies, 11
    buying land, 13
    camps, building, 15
    land, effects on, 89, 99
    and local economies, 101
    mills, delivery to, 71
    and reforestation, 109
logging crews, 20–28, **21, 25, 28, 30, 54**
    barn bosses, 22
    blacksmiths, 22–23, **22**
    bookkeepers/clerks, 23
    buckers, 24
    choppers, 24
    clothing, 29–30
    cookees, 23, 30–31, **31**
    cooks, 23, 30–31, **31**
    fitters, 24
    food for, 29–33
    foremen, 23–24
    immigrants, 20
    lumberjacks, 24, **24, 28, 90**
    markers, 24, **44, 45**
    Native loggers, 22
    payment, 26
    saw filers, 24
    scalers, 25
    skidders, 25
    swampers, 25
    teamsters, 25
logging equipment, 116–117
logging industry
    cutover land, 89–101
    decline, 99–101
    demand for wood, 10–11, 91
    Menominee Nation, 119
    peak years, 91
    sawdust towns, 78–79
    steam power, impact of, 86–87
    sustainable logging practices, 109, 121
logging roads, 43, **115**
logging trucks, 117, **117**
logjams, 61–65, **63, 65**
    Wisconsin River, 65–66
log rolling, 79, **79**
log scalers, 44
lumber contrasted with timber, 8
lumberjacks, 24, **24**, 28. *See also* logging crews
    free time, 46–51, **46, 47**
    working day, 45

Lumberjack World Championships, 79
lumber rafts, 66–69, **67**

M

Mackinaws (coats), 30
markers, 24
McNeel, Wakelin, 124–125, **125**
Menominee Nation, 2, 6–7
    logging practices, 118–120
    Menominee forest, **122**
    sawmill, 119–120
    women in forestry, **121**
Menominee reservation, 118
Menominee Tribal Enterprises, 119–120
mill ponds, 71
millwrights, 71
muley saws, 75
music, 47, **47**

N

national and state forests, 122–123
    map of, **124**
Native peoples, 2
    relationship with nature, 2–3
    rights to harvest trees, 119

sustainable forestry practices, 118–121
trading with Europeans, 4
treaties with US government, 6–7, 13
Neopit, Wisconsin, 119
night booms, 58

O

Oconto Falls, Wisconsin, 86
Ojibwe people, 2, 7, 22
Oshkosh, Chief, 118, **118**, 120
Oshkosh, Wisconsin, 78, 86
outhouses, 17
oxen, 25, **25**, **41**

P

Paul Bunyan, 50–51, **50**, **51**
peaveys, 55, **55**
Perkins, Frances, 114–115
Peshtigo, Wisconsin, 86
"The Peshtigo Brook Song," 47
Peshtigo Fire, 93–95, **93**
    map of, **94**
pike poles, 54
pit saws, 75
primary sources
    log hauler's experiences, 87
    logjam postcard, 65

lumberjack's letter, 27
lumberjack songs, 47
memories of the tote wagon, 32
postcards to recruit farmers, 103
raftsman's experiences, 68–69
what primary sources are, 26
women in logging camps, 35–36
public vs. private land, 118
pulley systems, 43

R

railroads, 82–83
"reading a tree," 38
reforestation, 107–109, **109**, 110, 111–113
renewable resources, 111
Rhinelander, Wisconsin, 48–49
rivers
    Black River, 78
    Chippewa River, 62, 65, 78
    currents in, 62
    dams, 62
    Fox River, 78
    logjams, 61–65
    map of, **53**

river highways, 52–54, 55
Rock River, 78
and sawmill locations, **53**, 78
St. Croix River, 64, 78
Wisconsin River, 65–67, **67**, 68–69, **70**, 78
Wolf River, 32, 78, 118
Roosevelt, Eleanor, 115
Roosevelt, Franklin D., 113
Roth, Filbert, 97
Russell, Harry, 123–124, 125

S

sash saws, 75
sawdust towns, 78–79
saw filers, 24, 72
sawmills, ix, **70**, 70–79, **76**
    dangers, 74
    debarking process, 72–73
    foremen, 71
    impacts of, 96
    map of, **53**
    mill ponds, 71
    millwrights, 71
    saw filers, 72
    sawyers, 72
    scalers, 72
    steam-powered, 85–86
    water turbine-powered mills, 74
    waterwheels, 73, **73**

saws
    band saws, 78, **78**
    chainsaws, 116–117
    circular saws, 76, **77**
    crosscut saws, 38, **39**, **41**
    gang saws, 76–77
    muley saws, 75
    pit saws, 75
    sash saws, 75
sawyers, 72
scalers, 25, 72
school forests, 123–125
settlers, European, 4–6, 10
shelterbelts, 112
Shepard, Eugene, 49
She-She-She camps, 114–115
skidders, 25
skidding tongs/trees, 39–40, **40**
sleds, 41–42, **42**
softwood, 12, 120
stamps/marks, 44–45, **44**, **45**
state forests, 123, **123**, 124
    map of, **124**
steam power
    impact on lumber industry, 86–87
    sawmills, 85–86
    steamboats, 81, **81**
    steam engines, 80–81

steam log haulers, 84–85, **84**
steam-powered trains, 82–83, **82**, **85**, **137**
stewardship, 131–132, **132**, 135–136
stores in logging camps, 18
stump removal, 104–105, **104**, **105**
Sunday chores, 51, **51**
sustainable forestry, 121–122
swampers, 25

T

tall tales, 48–51
teamsters, 25
"Timber!" call, ix
timber contrasted with lumber, 8
timber cruisers, 13–15
tools. *See also* saws
    anvils, 18
    augers, 66, **66**
    axes, 37
    cant hooks, 42
    peaveys, 55, **55**
    pike poles, 54
    pulley systems, 43
    skidding tongs, 39–40, **40**
topsoil, 96

tote wagons, 32
trains, steam-powered, 82–83, **82**, **85**
tree canopy, 129
tree nurseries, 108, 109, **109**
trees
    deciduous vs. coniferous, 12, **12**, 120
    felling, 37–39
    skidding, 39–40
    species, 120
    value and impact, 126–131, 133
trees, planting. *See* reforestation
Trotier, Iva, 34–36
Trout Lake Nursery, 108, 109, **109**

U

Urban Roots volunteers, **132**

W

wanigans, 58-59, **59**
water turbine-powered mills, 74
waterwheels, 73, **73**
Weyerhaeuser, Frederick, 123
white pine trees
    demand for, 10–11
    forests, ix, 1
    height, 39
    as lumber, 8–9
    and Wisconsin's soil and climate, 11
wildlife, 2, 4, 95, 118, 127, **128**
winter weather, 21
Wisconsin
    forest conditions (1897), **98**
    map of forests before logging era, **9**
    map of state forests today, **124**
    state forests, 123–124
    statehood, 7
    as territory, 6–7
Wisconsin Conservation Department, 113
Wisconsin River, 65–66
    lumber rafting, 66–67, **67**
Wisconsin Supreme Court, 109
Wolf River, 118
women
    in logging camps, 34–36, **34**
    Menominee women in forestry, 121, **121**
    She-She-She camps, 114–115
World War II, 114
Wyalusing State Park, 114

Z

Ziebarth, John, 27
zoning laws, 110–111

About the Authors

SUSAN APPS-BODILLY is a retired elementary and middle-school educator. She is the author of *One Room Schools: Stories from the Days of 1 Room, 1 Teacher, 8 Grades*; *Seeds in Soil: Planting a Garden and Finding Your Roots*; and coauthor, with Jerry Apps, of *Old Farm County Cookbook*, all published by the Wisconsin Historical Society Press. Susan and her husband, Paul, have four children and three grandchildren. She enjoys gardening, kayaking, and spending time hiking in the woods at the family tree farm, Roshara, in Waushara County.

JERRY APPS is a former county extension agent and professor emeritus for the College of Agriculture and Life Science at the University of Wisconsin–Madison. Today he works as a rural historian and full-time writer. Jerry is the author of more than forty fiction, nonfiction, and children's books with topics ranging from barns, cranberries, cucumbers, and cheese factories to farming with horses and the Civilian Conservation Corps. He and his wife, Ruth, have three children, seven grandchildren, and three great grandchildren. They divide their time between their home in Madison and their tree farm, Roshara, in Waushara County.

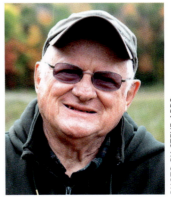